A MOONLIT KNIGHT

A KNIGHTS THROUGH TIME ROMANCE

CYNTHIA LUHRS

For all of you who believe in fairy tales.

CHAPTER 1

"THIS IS SUPPOSED to be the happiest day of our lives and you look like somebody swiped your last piece of peach pie."

Chloe fingered the green and white tassel. It looked like Christmas lying on the red table. "I am happy."

"Chloe Penelope Merriweather, don't you dare fib to me." Sara Beth scowled across the table, green eyes bright under the neon signs.

It was loud in the diner. Everyone from school had gathered together one last time before they partied all night long and went their separate ways over the summer. Chloe sighed.

"Really. Truly. I'm happy."

Her friend was gorgeous, with green eyes and short black hair. She'd be perfect on a movie poster about an escaped fae princess. Half of the baseball team was drooling as they watched Sara Beth eat her sweet potato fries.

She waved a fry in the air, ketchup droplets landing on the table. "Oh, please. I'm positive you're having some kind of crisis. I mean, come on, you turned down *Jake Evans*, the hottest guy in three counties. Something's up." She narrowed her eyes. "Now spill."

Stalling for time, Chloe took a long sip of the double chocolate shake. Then she reapplied her lip balm and looked around the diner. It was retro; the waitstaff dressed like they were from the fifties.

Sara Beth's mom was a life coach and her best friend loved to analyze and "help" those around her. Though right now, Chloe could do without her friend's all-seeing gaze. She forced herself not to squirm but to remain relaxed and cheerful. A senior graduating from high school. Going onward, ready to start the rest of her entire life and plan everything out down to the last detail. Oh my gosh, was it hot in here? Chloe fanned herself.

A sharp rap on the table made her jump. "What?"

"I swear if you don't tell me what's going on, I'm going to text Jake this instant and tell him you're on the way to his party." Sara Beth held up her phone, the purple glitter case sparkling under the lights.

The anxiety of knowing what to do with the rest of her life faded a bit and Chloe laughed, holding out her hands. "Okay, okay, you win."

Her friend leaned across the table. "Is that it? You've reconsidered?"

"No way." Chloe shook her head. "Jake is hot, I'll give you that much, but he's dated every girl within a hundred miles. I'm not interested in being another ex of Jake Evans. There should be a support group. They could call it Jake's Jilted Women." How did she explain to her best friend what she was having trouble figuring out herself?

"We're done with high school. You're going to California for the summer and then UCLA. Everyone's leaving. Nothing will ever be the same again. Before you know it, we'll all be back here for our twenty-year reunion and everyone will be so much older. I want time to stop."

Sara Beth took her hand and squeezed. "Everything is supposed to change. We're going to college and then we'll find jobs, get married, maybe have a couple of kids—who knows where we'll end up living. You have to keep moving forward. It's just life." Then she grinned. "But I'm not aging. No way. I plan to look like this forever."

Chloe sniffed. "I know we have to grow up. But why can't things stay the same?" She blew her nose. "Don't get me wrong; I'm super excited to travel around Europe. But my grandparents are getting older. I thought they'd be here forever, constant, never changing." Her throat closed up and Chloe had to swallow a few times before she could go on.

"They're supposed to be here forever. Arthur is nice enough and my mom is great, but Granda Drake is the one I want to walk me down the aisle, to pull out his sword and tell the guy he better treat me right or he'll run him through." The words tumbled out, faster and faster. "When I think of losing them, I can't breathe. What if something happens to one of them while I'm gone this summer? Or away at school?" She used her thumb to swipe at the tear rolling down her cheek.

Sara Beth squeezed her hand, then let go. "You've been my best friend since third grade, when you socked Willie James for putting that awful toad down the back of my dress." She paused while the waitress cleared their plates.

"Can I get y'all anything else? Everyone's heading to the Evans' for the big party."

Chloe let out a long sigh.

"No thanks, Mrs. Bean. Just the check," Sara Beth said.

Mrs. Bean hugged them, tightly. The woman was a workout fanatic with arms of steel. "This one's on me. You only graduate from high school once. Now you two have fun tonight."

When they were alone again, Sara Beth looked Chloe in the eye. "Everyone in town knows your grandmother will live forever. My mom says Miss Mildred has mellowed but that she used to terrorize the whole town before she and Drake got together."

"She almost fell on the steps last week," Chloe said. "And now she's hobbling around. It makes my heart hurt."

"Girl, you trip over your own feet at least once a week. And Miss Mildred will outlive us all." Sara Beth stopped laughing. "You've always been serious. With your nose in a book, daydreaming away. But Chloe, it's time to take your nose out of the book, forget the imaginary boyfriends, and live. Fall in love with a real guy. Someone a little older than you. You need a guy who's mature and responsible. Someone who cares about others more than himself."

"I've been in love," Chloe retorted.

Sara Beth smirked. "Oh, you have, have you?" She pointed at a group of guys in the corner. "And what fine specimen of manhood has had the honor of your affections?"

"Well…Mike."

"Please. You dumped him for not holding the door open for you."

"Fine. I loved Jim."

Sara Beth rolled her eyes. "You said kissing him was like getting big, slobbery, smelly kisses from a dog."

"There was—"

"That's what I thought. You hold every guy up to an impossible level. No guy will ever measure up to Mr. Drake. Or to any book boyfriend." Sara Beth arched a brow.

"Noah," Chloe whispered.

"Oh, sweetie." Sara Beth took her hand, the purple nail polish sparkling in the light. "I know you loved him. I'm an idiot for bringing the subject up."

"It's taken me a long time to get over him." Chloe pulled her hand away. "When you and Bobby broke up, how long did it take you to trust again?"

Sara Beth looked away. "I'm still working on it." Then she smiled. "But I'm dating, and I'll keep dating until I know I'm over it. By then, I'll be ridiculously happy."

"It's hard for me to put myself out there," Chloe said as she slid out of the booth.

"I know. But if you don't, you'll end up all alone with five little yappy dogs that you dress up in costumes and post all over social media." Sara Beth hugged Chloe as they made their way out of the diner. It was nearly empty; everyone was already on their way to the party.

"Promise me." Sara Beth pulled back and looked Chloe in the eye. "Promise me you'll give some cute, slightly older European guy a chance, and fall madly in love with him. You need a summer fling. Or better yet, a fling in every country." She waggled her eyebrows, looking like a demented fairy.

"That's ridiculous," Chloe said. "Why would I want to fall in love and then have to come back to the States and go away to college in the fall? I think that's a bit too long-distance of a relationship, even for me."

"Trust me. You'll hear all those sexy accents and fall in love. It will be good for you. Consider it homework." Sara Beth climbed into the passenger seat of the red MG. "I still can't believe Miss Mildred let you take the car tonight. Now put your hair up and let's go find a cute boy to kiss to celebrate graduating. With honors, I might add."

Instead of retorting that she'd kissed enough frogs for several lifetimes, Chloe put her hair up and then put the top down on the old car. She'd make an appearance at the party and talk Sara Beth into leaving early.

Her friend cranked up the radio, singing along, and Chloe gave up that plan. It was going to be a long night.

CHAPTER 2

SUMMER 1334—ENGLAND

"Nay, we must go around." The warrior crossed himself.

Another agreed. "'Tis a cursed place."

"Bloody hell," Richard said. "'Tis as if I am besieged by Garrick's seven sisters instead of seasoned warriors. I've no patience for sniveling women."

Richard FitzGregory, now Lord Bainford, dismounted with a grunt, his leg giving way as he went down on one knee. One of his men rushed to his aid as he cursed. "Leave me be. My leg was stiff from riding so long." He pulled the hood of his cloak up, covering the side of his face.

Much as he was loath to admit, the standing stones were fearsome. A presence lingered, not unlike walking across a battlefield long after the battle was over. With a grim look at the stones, he hesitated, hearing whispers where there were no men. Mayhap they should go around.

Garrick clapped him on the shoulder. "My lord, shall we go around? 'Tis said the wood is not haunted as this wicked place."

"Cease calling me 'my lord,'" Richard grumbled.

His captain smiled. "But, Lord Bainford, 'tis your title, granted by the king." Garrick wisely took a step back. "Mayhap you should not have saved his life. Though methinks a title and a castle 'tis a proper trade for your pretty visage and your eye."

Garrick ignored the look of displeasure as his incessant babbling, never-ending, seeped into Richard's skull. He had the intense need to throttle his oldest friend.

"Your face before the arrow found its mark was not so pleasing. Now you look rather like a pirate. Lasses like pirates." Then Garrick chuckled. "Mayhap 'tis the pirate's gold lasses desire, not the pirate."

"All men look alike in the dark," another of the men called out.

"Says you," Richard said. "All the lasses can tell me from you womanly lot."

There were jeers and slurs from the men, each more outlandish than the last.

"Cease," Richard said. He stomped about, cursing and snarling until his foul mood improved. Wisely, the men were closemouthed, tending to the horses.

The horses were fresh, the weather mild, the stones a day's ride from Bainford Castle. There were black rumors about the place. 'Twas said to be haunted. He snorted. The perfect place for a man with his affliction. A beast.

"My lord?" One of the men nervously looked about. "Might we continue our journey?"

With a sigh, Richard allowed he would have to accept being addressed as "my lord." Perchance 'twas better than being called bastard or monster. Which he was, thanks to his father and to the enemy who'd failed to murder his king. Richard wished his wretched father was still breathing so he could run him through.

"Come. Let us leave this cursed place and sleep with a roof over our heads, cold ale, and warm wenches this night, lads."

The men were silent as they rode past the stones. Richard sneered. He would show no fear. In saving the life of his king, Richard had not escaped unscathed; he'd lost an eye and the fire had taken half of his visage. As he was healing in an abandoned chapel, the roof collapsed, and he almost lost his leg and arm. Injured and deformed, he was awarded a title, a castle, and sent away. There would be no more enemies for him to vanquish. No more battles to be fought. A cripple was useless. Richard's men were granted leave by their sire to see him home safely as if he were a mere child. Did his sovereign see fit to gift him gold? Nay. So Richard hoped his home would not require any repair, as his own gold was in short supply. He cast a dark look over his shoulder at the stones.

"Not like my life could be any worse." Thunder cracked across the sky, his horse galloped into the woods, and Richard swore he heard the sound of laughter over the storm.

The forest opened to a clearing, and from there they could see Bainford Castle. Richard could not fathom that this was to be his home. Until they rode closer. The walls were crumbling, bits of rubble strewn about, and as they rode under the portcullis, he swallowed, the walls closing in on him, the journey lasting a fortnight, until finally they rode into the gloomy courtyard.

Saints, the place was little more than a ruin. The door to his hall hung open and birds took flight from holes in the roof.

Garrick raised a meaty hand and scratched at his chin. "I thought it would be—"

"Nay, do not say. 'Tis an ill-fated day." Richard looked to the heavens and around the bailey. "Tell me the stables are intact."

The grim look on the men's faces told him the tidings were not good.

"There are only a few holes in the walls and roof." The man grimaced as the rain pounded the ground. "The garrison is the same, my lord."

"Bloody hell." Richard pushed the hood back, the rain cooling his face, and ran a hand through his hair. "See to the horses." He unsheathed his sword, relishing a challenge, no matter how small. "I will see to the hall."

Feeling every bit his score of years, Richard entered the gloom, prepared to do battle with whatever evil lurked within.

"ARE YE JUST GETTING IN?" Drake Montgomery, or Granda, as Chloe called him, handed her a mug of green tea.

"I know, right? A cup of tea will wake me up."

Her granda ran a hand through his hair as Chloe squinted up at him.

"Sara Beth decided to stay at the party. I left early and walked on the beach. Guess I fell asleep out here." She yawned and stretched. "What time is it? My phone died."

He sat in one of the rocking chairs, next to her, facing the water.

"Do you remember when you were little, Millie and I would find you out here, curled up in a chair with that tattered stuffed elephant you carried everywhere? Your poor mom would be frantic looking for you."

"I remember. Ellie was my best friend. Mom sewed her up so many times she looked like Frankenstein. I still have her; she's on my bookshelf."

Chloe scraped her corkscrew curls back into a long ponytail. How was it possible? During the school year, days seemed to take weeks to pass, while time with Drake and Mildred, whom he called Millie, passed in seconds. They weren't her real grandparents, but they'd adopted her mom and Chloe, so to her they were as real as any biological family. Maybe more so, because they'd chosen her.

"You better text your mom and let her know you're here."

"Let me plug in. The phone died." After a few minutes, she had enough charge and saw there were several missed calls from her mom.

Nope. Not calling right now. Chloe knew her mom was not happy about the upcoming trip, and she was too tired to fight about it before she had even eaten breakfast. Taking the easy way out, she sent off a quick text to let Mom know she was at Gull Cottage.

She and her mom, and now Arthur, lived a few streets down. They had a view of the marsh, but there was something about the ocean, hearing the waves, and watching the ebb and flow of the tide that always helped Chloe think.

"Done." She put the phone on the table and rocked back and forth, happy to sit in silence with her granda and watch the gulls play in the waves.

❦

RICHARD SAT ON A STOOL, his feet warm from the fire in the hearth as the wind howled outside like the very hounds of hell he was oft compared to.

He knew what was said about him in the village. In truth, he had not meant to become a recluse. Tired of being called a beast, he retreated within his walls, such as they were, and brooded. A great deal. Though he also drank ale when he could not fathom what his life had come to. Thus far, it had been a tragedy of immense proportions.

His arm and leg pained him nigh unto death, no matter how he shifted on the stool to ease the pain or how many cups of ale he consumed.

A year had passed since his wounding, and his temper was as foul as the day it happened. Richard reached under the black fabric, gently touching the scars covering the side of his face. The raised skin rough under his fingers as he traced the lines down the side of his ruined visage. The wounds had healed, though he was still broken. He should go to the lists, but could not bestir himself to move.

"My lord, I've brought you wine with herbs from the healer. She says you need to go outside every day. And you must eat."

"You drink it, old man," Richard told his steward. "Leave me be and cease your incessant babbling."

Edwin left the wine, hobbling out of the hall, stooped over but moving faster than Richard on his best days. He remembered, nigh on a year ago, brandishing his sword as he entered his new home, only to come face to face with the man. The old man had peered up at him and shuffled deeper into the gloom. Edwin had refused to leave, said he was born at Bainford and would die at Bainford, and did his lordship want supper or no?

Richard drank the foul brew, sat alone in the hall, and kept company with his black thoughts.

The door opened with a bang, cold wind blew through his hall, and Richard swore as he spilled the ale.

"Smells like you have been sleeping with the pigs." Garrick stood before him, mighty hands on his hips, looking most pleased.

"Bloody hell. Can a man not brood in peace?"

Garrick sniffed. "Nay, I was wrong. Pigs smell better than you." Then he grinned as Richard gained his footing. "Come have a go at me in the lists. You will find your mood improved." Garrick laughed. "Or mayhap your mood will turn as black as the night when I best you for all to see."

Richard faltered. "All?"

"Aye. I brought men to repair your walls, dolt."

"Where, pray tell, did you acquire these warriors amongst men that would brave the wrath of the monster of Bainford?" Richard fixed him with a grim look.

"Ireland."

Richard blinked. Then he laughed, the sound like an old iron gate that had been unused for years. A serving girl dropped the wash and ran out the door, back to the safety of the laundry, leaving the sodden heap of wash on the floor of his hall.

"Bloody hell, girl," he said.

"She is but a child, Richard." Garrick placed a hand on his shoulder. "Come. Let us see if you have forgotten how to wield a sword."

Once the cloak and hood were fastened securely, Richard limped outside, blinking in the weak sunlight.

Edwin called out to the few servants brave enough to serve the beast. "Into the hall, the lot of you. I've work needs doing and no time for idleness."

Richard did not allow a soul to watch him in the lists as he removed his cloak and hood. In truth, it wounded his pride to hear the gasps and muffled prayers, to see his servants crossing themselves.

No one spoke a word of the doings at Bainford, for if they did, they would find themselves turned out at the gates. Though to hear the village tales, he would mount their heads on pikes for all to see. Richard rolled his eyes. Anyone could see there were no heads mounted on his gates. He snorted. *Because he eats them,* the villagers would whisper as they crossed themselves and prayed for their immortal souls.

The way his leg pained him, Richard knew snow was coming. The bleak landscape, the steel-colored sky, and the brisk air much improved his mood. The weak sunlight did little to warm him, but he did not care. A bit of swordplay would have him sweating soon enough.

Three of the lads from Ireland flinched as he removed the cloak. Two crossed themselves, and Richard marked them.

"You." He unsheathed his sword. "Shall we begin?"

Garrick chuckled and settled on a bench set against the wall. "A bit of swordplay will leave you lads weary. You'll fall asleep in your cups and leave all the wenches to me. Fighting is as important as stonework. Don't go easy on his lordship."

Saints, they were inept. Richard spent the day throttling the men until they were leaning against the wall or sitting on the ground, panting. He hoped their masonry skills were better than their swordplay.

"Is there no one else?" He waved his sword about, the muscles in his arm flexing as he lunged and then winced. His leg and arm pained him. "Take your ease, lads. Tonight you sleep in the garrison, and on the morrow, work."

Garrick made a show of shivering. "'Tis about time. I thought my feet had fallen off. Let us partake of the fine wine in your cellars."

Hrmph. "How long are you staying? You eat and drink enough for a score of men. My larder will not see me through the winter."

Garrick chuckled. "You forget. I've seen your cellar and your larder. I could feast here for nigh on a year." He made a show of looking around, his heavy treads following Richard as they entered the hall. "Still no wife. The hall smells like a cesspit."

"Be silent, dolt. What sire would plight his daughter's troth with the Beast of Bainford?"

"One who cares for gold and title," Garrick retorted.

Richard snorted. "Not bloody likely. I've sent missives to every eligible maiden in England. None will have me."

"There's always Ireland, or perhaps Italy?"

Richard rolled his eyes. "No more talk of wenches." He would not tell Garrick how he'd beseeched the fates to send him a wife. How his heart wrenched inside his chest when he thought of her looking upon his form, disgust in her eyes. The same way he looked upon his own visage in the still waters of the lake.

He was a monster, and monsters did not take wives.

CHAPTER 3

"WHAT'S GOING ON? Everyone looks so serious." Chloe set the groceries on the counter, careful not to crush the bread, then turned to face her family. Gram looked like she was trying not to laugh, while Granda tapped his fingers against his hip. The man fidgeted. A lot. Her mom had "the look," so Chloe busied herself putting away groceries to buy a little time and try and figure out what was going on.

While Gram was perfectly capable of doing her own grocery shopping, Chloe liked to run errands for her. Her mom was busy with her business, so Chloe had taken over doing the shopping for them both.

Gram was turning eighty this year and still drove her big car and the little MG. The donations to the local police department had grown larger over the years, though nothing could top the year Granda donated a helicopter on Gram's seventy-fifth birthday.

"We want to talk about your trip." Her mom looked at Arthur, Chloe's stepdad for the past eight years. A look passed between them, and Chloe knew what was coming as she put the empty plastic bags in the walk-in pantry.

"I'm all ready to go. Checked all my lists twice." The huge windows in the great room beckoned, and she found herself looking out at the ocean, rather than at her mom, who meant well but took worrying to the expert level.

Trying to prepare for the coming argument, Chloe took deep breaths and waited. Her temper, her mom said, had come from her dad. Not that she knew much about him, just the basics. What he looked like, his name, and, oh yeah, that he hadn't wanted either one of them. He'd left her mom at the local Dollar Store, pregnant and homeless. The jerk.

Granda Drake had been father and grandfather to Chloe for her entire life. Just because someone shared DNA with you, didn't make them a parent.

Restless, Chloe turned and went to the kitchen. "Who wants a glass of tea?" The tea was always sweet here in the South—no need to ask for sweet or unsweet.

"I do, dearie," Gram said.

"Me too, with a bit of mint," Granda chimed in.

"No thanks, honey." Her mom and Arthur had bottles of water in front of them and exchanged another look.

Nervous at the coming upheaval, Chloe added lemon wedges and brought the tray over, sitting next to Granda. He winked and took a glass of tea, passing it to Gram before taking his own glass.

"Okay, Karen," Chloe said. "What's to discuss? Everything is paid for, I've exchanged a bit of money, I'm all packed, and I leave *tomorrow*."

Karen—Chloe liked to call her mom by her name when she was mad at her—pressed her lips together. "You know how I feel about that, young lady."

Wisely, Chloe didn't respond. Instead, she rolled her eyes and waited, her bare foot tapping up and down.

Arthur patted Karen's hand. "It's just with the state of the world right now, we thought it might be better if you spent your summer here." He smoothed his tie down. "Not here in Holden Beach but somewhere in the U.S. Maybe California or Maine?"

"We don't want you traipsing around Europe all by yourself," Karen said.

"I'll meet plenty of people traveling alone at the hostels. Kids from Australia take their gap year and travel alone all the time. No one tells them the world isn't safe. The world will never be safe. I'm not a child. I'll be careful."

Unwilling to lose this battle, Chloe pulled out the big guns.

"Gram?" Chloe turned pleading eyes to the woman who scared half the town with her prickly demeanor, but Chloe knew that inside she was a big, soft marshmallow.

"The trip *is* paid for, Karen," Gram said. "And Drake added international calling to the plan on her phone so she can keep in touch."

When her mom jumped up and started pacing, Chloe tuned out and waited for the heated discussion to end. Granda nudged her and leaned in close, whispering, "Your gram and I are on your side. After all, aren't grandparents supposed to spoil their grandkids?"

Chloe wanted to hug him, but didn't dare in case her mom noticed. The back-and-forth died down and her mom let out a long sigh.

"I don't like it, but fine." Karen looked at Arthur and then to Chloe. "You'll call us twice a day."

It took considerable effort for Chloe not to roll her eyes. Fine—she knew how to negotiate, thanks to Granda. After all, he used to run one of the biggest casinos in Las Vegas.

"Once a week."

"That is not acceptable." Karen fumed.

"Once every two weeks, then," Chloe countered.

"How about when you land and then every day?" her stepdad said. Arthur was an accountant. Chloe and Gram thought Karen picked him because he was stable and kind, if a bit boring. Gram said Karen had been hurt so deeply that she wanted someone with his feet firmly planted on the ground.

A small snort escaped Chloe. Her stepdad was nice, she'd give him that, but he couldn't tell a good fairy tale to save his life. She hugged her granda. Now, he had the best stories, probably because most of them were true.

"This is my last summer to be a kid and have fun before I buckle down at college this fall," Chloe said. "And then it's working every day for the next forty years. I don't want to have to call my mama every day." She smiled to ease the sting of the words.

"Hear me out." Chloe stood and moved across the room to perch on the arm of the loveseat where her parents presented a united front. "I'll call when I land and then I'll call when I leave and arrive in each country. If I decide to stay in one country, I'll call when I visit each city."

"Sounds reasonable, don't you agree, Karen?" Granda said, his deep voice filling the room.

"You know I love you, Drake," Karen said. "But you and Mildred have filled Chloe's head with fairy tales ever since she was born. I worry she won't pay attention to her surroundings and will end up getting kidnapped or mugged."

Gram leaned forward. "Come now, dearie. You've been watching too much news and all those awful crime shows. Chloe is a responsible young woman. Soon enough she'll be on her own. It'll be good for her to spread her wings a bit. And if I remember, *you* were eighteen when you came to live with me."

Oh boy, Karen was mad as hops. Chloe could always tell because her mom jiggled her shoe back and forth. *Slap. Slap. Slap.*

A look passed between her parents, and her mom finally sighed, looking older than her thirty-eight years.

"Okay. You free spirits win. Call when you land. And each time you head to a new place." She narrowed her eyes. "If we don't hear from you, I will hire someone to track you down and drag you back, embarrassing you and scarring you for life. Deal?"

"Deal." Chloe hugged her. "Thanks, Mom and Dad." Then she sat between her grandparents and hugged them both close, whispering, "I knew you could get her to see reason."

Granda leaned in. "Come upstairs later. I've got a present for you before you leave."

Chloe jumped up. "This is going to be the trip of a lifetime."

"I'll be tracking your phone," her mom muttered.

"What did you say?" Chloe couldn't quite make out the words.

"We'll be counting down the days until you come back, honey." Her mom smiled, and Chloe frowned but let it go.

Tomorrow she was leaving to spend the entire summer in Europe. And while she'd told her parents she was traveling all around, the truth was that she was spending all her time in England. She'd tell her mom when she landed that she'd decided to stay and really get to know Granda's country. It was also where Gram's nieces had vanished.

Maybe the reason she'd failed all these years was that she hadn't been in England when she'd tried her experiments. Excitement coursed through her, only to be replaced with crushing defeat. No, Chloe had put childish fairy tales away after the last fiasco when she was ten. Time travel might be real for the special few, but she wasn't a "real" Merriweather, and deep down she knew: time travel just wasn't in the cards.

❧

RICHARD STOOD on the battlements watching the men. 'Twas good to have men about, shouting slurs at each other as they worked to repair his walls and his home.

A fortnight had passed, and while a few still crossed themselves, the rest of the men accepted him. no longer flinching when they saw him with his hood down.

"Are you going back to France?" he said to Garrick, who looked as weary as Richard.

"Aye. I left word for any missives to be delivered to Bainford. Mayhap the messenger is too afeared of the monster to darken your hall."

Richard ignored the jest. Garrick was a score and five. A huge man, with scarred hands the size of silver dinner plates. Richard had saved his life when they were but lads, and since then, Garrick had gone wherever Richard went.

"Why are you not yet married? Surely you can find a lass willing to bed ye?" Richard knew the lasses flocked to his friend.

"Between fighting and watching over your reckless self, who has time to seek a wife?" Garrick retorted. "We are both bastards, Richard. And whilst you have title and lands, I do not. What woman of worth would have me?"

"If 'tis because your home is here at Bainford, I would see you settled elsewhere where rumor does not reach." Richard brushed the lightly falling snow from his cloak, grateful for its warmth.

Garrick turned to him. "Nay. Who would look after your sorry self?" He grinned. "And while the lads are doing fine work repairing the stone, my home is in England. Here at Bainford. Not in Ireland. Do not worry over me." He shuddered.

Richard nodded. "Enough womanly talk. To the lists?"

"Aye, I thought ye'd never ask."

CHAPTER 4

HEATHROW WAS BUSTLING as Chloe cleared customs, her luggage in tow. She'd carried on her small bag, planning to take advantage of the laundry offered at most hostels. After thinking about it, she'd decided to come clean with her mom. They thought she'd be traveling all over Europe instead of spending all her time in England. Chloe had been so sure her parents would tell her not to believe all of Granda's stories, and she didn't want to hear it, so she'd made up the whole "visit a ton of countries" itinerary.

During the flight she'd decided her mom would be happier knowing she was spending all her time in one country, and Chloe would feel better knowing she wasn't deceiving them. If they started in on their tired "not romanticizing the past" talk, she'd tune them out like she did when she got lost in a good book.

The black lightweight trench coat with the pink polka dot lining kept her dry. Normally she hated rain, it made her curls extra springy, but here? The light drizzle made the day picture perfect.

The bus to take her to the hostel would be here shortly, so she called her mom while she waited. A couple of guys with Australian accents smiled, and she tripped over her bag, feeling like an idiot. Had they smiled because of the outfit or because they thought she was cute? Chloe wished she was pretty like Sara Beth instead of plain and average. Boring and quiet.

Mean girl Caroline made sure everyone knew boring, bookish Chloe. So she preferred books to people—why did Caroline have to be so judgmental? It wasn't like Chloe judged Miss Meanie on her shallow personality.

"Hello? Chloe?"

"Sorry. Hi, Mom. I'm here. In England."

"Arthur, come here. It's Chloe. I'm putting you on speaker."

She turned to face the airport, glad the gathering tour group couldn't hear her talking to her mommy.

"How long will you be in England, honey?"

"For the whole summer."

There was a moment of silence, and then her mom was talking a hundred miles a minute.

"We're so glad you'll be in one country. Much safer. Be careful. Watch out for muggers. Always watch your drinks when you're out. Boys will put roofies in your drink. Keep your money and passport hidden. Do you need anything? Did you bring enough clean underwear? Where are you going first?"

"Mom. Stop." Geez, so many questions. "I'm taking a tour around London with a group and staying in a hostel for a week or two. When I figure out where I'm going next, I'll call, okay?"

"I'll tell Mildred and Drake. They're planning to spend a couple of weeks in the mountains, at the lake house one of those rich executive types your grandfather trains with swords owns." She heard muffled talking before her mom came back. "I have no idea why anyone would want to swing a sword around. It's so silly. Technology is where it's at. Did I tell you I picked up a new client? The vet in town wants me to manage their social media. Isn't that great?"

"Great." It was easier to answer her mom's last question and ignore the rest. Sometimes it was hard to keep up with her mom. Her conversations jumped all over the place. Unbelievable when she was so organized with her business. She'd started out creating websites for local businesses and then branched out to running their social media.

Chloe didn't have the heart to tell her mom that her grandparents already knew the plan and that she'd texted them to let them know she arrived safely. They talked for a bit longer, and Chloe felt better, knowing her mom wouldn't worry. She snorted. That was an exaggeration—of course her mom would worry, but not as much as if Chloe had been traveling all around the world. Next summer, maybe she'd take a trip to India or Australia. The guys from down under didn't seem to care she was plain.

"I love you guys. I'll miss you both."

"Love you, honey. Have fun and be safe." Chloe could hear Arthur in the background asking if she had enough money and if she'd brought an umbrella. He was so practical, and her mom adored him. They were a good match, even if he was a little boring. Then again, Chloe was boring, so what did she know?

"Miss? The bus is leaving. You coming?"

"Oh, right. Sorry." Chloe wheeled her suitcase over so the guy could put it in the baggage hold. On the bus, there were about twenty kids, and she guessed they ranged from her age to twenty-five. Everyone was friendly enough, chatting away as the guide pointed out the sights. It was going to be a great summer. Maybe Sara Beth was right—maybe Chloe needed to kiss a few boys. Have a fling.

No. She wrinkled her nose. She wasn't the fling type, but a kiss or three would be okay.

As she shifted in the seat, something clinked, and she put her hand in the inside pocket of her trench, touching the bag Granda had given her before she'd left. He'd called her upstairs and handed her a bag of old coins. "Not like you could spend them. More to bring you the favor of the fates."

Then he'd winked at her. "You never know what the fates have planned."

"MY LORD, RIDERS APPROACH." The newest man to join Richard's small guard stood before him, looking at the ground. As the seasons passed, winter had given way to spring, the snow replaced by green, and Richard found himself with seven men willing to serve him. He tried not to think overmuch on how long it took the men to look him in the eye.

No longer did he look upon his visage in still water—nay, he no longer cared what was said about him. And if he kept telling himself such untruths, mayhap in time he would come to believe 'twas true.

His steward spat on the ground. "More mouths to feed for supper." He called to the two serving girls who cleaned and took care of the laundry. As they had no cook, Edwin saw to the food. Richard put a hand to his gut, thinking on the barely edible fare that came from the kitchens. When they passed the overgrown garden, he sighed. 'Twas nigh impossible to find servants who did not cower in fear and run before their first night at Bainford passed.

In the courtyard, Richard tightened his hood and waited as the men approached.

One of the men held out a pouch, bulging with coin. "We come to best the Beast of Bainford." The trembling of his hand, the coins jingling, gave away his fear.

A sneer filled Richard's face. "And you?" He looked to the other man. "Have you too come to try your skill against me?"

The man swallowed. "Aye. I have." He held out a small bag of coin, and Richard frowned. "'Tis a paltry sum."

"My boy has eight summers, and the girl ten. They will work hard."

This man wanted to wager his children? Richard forced himself not to gape at the dolt. Instead, he shrugged.

"As you will." He stroked his chin, looking them over. "They are scrawny."

"Please. Don't eat us." The girl wept as her brother comforted her. "Don't cry, Merry. I won't leave ye."

"Enough. To the lists, where I shall relieve you of your gold."

The Irishmen stopped their labors, taking places along the walls, calling out wagers. A year ago, Richard would have not allowed any to watch him fight, but that was then. Now, he relished his role as monster. The gold he had won fighting men had paid for the repairs to his home.

The gasp when he removed his hood and cloak made Richard tighten his hand on the hilt of his sword. The hiss of the sword as it came free from the scabbard filled the air.

Mere moments later, 'twas over. These skirmishes were short-lived—the men lost their gold, went to drown their sorrows in the tavern, and told more and more outrageous tales about the beast and the evil doings at Bainford Castle.

One of his guard aided the two men in finding the gates, on foot. For Richard had taken their horses as well as their gold.

Once they were gone, he turned to face the children, the girl hiding behind her brother.

"Have you eaten?"

"Nay," the boy said. But he looked Richard in the eye and did not flinch.

"What are your names?"

The boy stood tall. "I am Robin." He pulled his sister next to him. "This is Merry." He whispered something to her, and she nodded. Impossibly blue eyes, the color of the North Sea, met his.

"I can cook and sew," she said.

"Edwin will be pleased." Richard clapped his hands together as the children jumped. "To the kitchens. You will eat, then my steward will show you where to sleep and what to do."

"Thank ye, my lord," the boy said.

"Are you not afeared of me?"

"Our father beat us. You cannot be worse," Merry said.

A rider could catch the man, bring him back to Richard. Nay, he would let the man go. Many beat their wives and children, though Richard did not. He had been beaten enough as a child that he would never lift a hand to the helpless and weak.

"Do your chores and speak to no one of the goings on at Bainford, and I will not beat you." He grinned at them. "Nor will I eat you. Come, let us fill our bellies."

§

THE NEXT MONTH FLEW BY. Chloe loved everything about England. The history, the accents, the vibe—it was all perfect. Even the rain was welcome. A ponytail had become her go-to hairstyle to keep the brown corkscrew curls tamed. She and two girls from Australia had been traveling together. The girls were funny, routinely making Chloe snort water out of her nose. They reminded her of Sara Beth. Her friend would be thrilled: Chloe had kissed one Brit and one Scot, so in her book, the trip was a success. It didn't really matter that the kisses were just kisses; she didn't feel them down to her toes, they didn't make her swoon, and no one swept her up onto his horse and carried her off to his castle.

If she didn't love books so much, she'd hate the authors for making her believe with every fiber of her being that a single kiss could change your life.

She'd let her family know she was off to spend a few weeks wandering around the Cotswolds. The area was like something out of a travel commercial, so picturesque that she never wanted to leave. The flowers were beautiful and the thatched cottages made her want to curl up in a garden with a book and wile the day away reading.

Yesterday, she and her new friends had gone on a guided walk and taken a tour of the area. There was a nearby lake perfect for swimming, and a castle ruin. Today she wanted to visit a stone circle she'd heard about last night: the Rollright Stones.

"Come on, go with me. It will be interesting, and afterwards drinks are on me at the pub. Please?" Chloe said.

"No way." Lola shook her head so hard that her sunglasses went flying into the street and were run over by a passing car.

Jules chimed in: "You heard the stories those girls from Japan told us last night down the pub. Sometimes the stones just disappear. Giant stones vanishing in the fog. I heard they practice witchcraft there. Even the guide said never to go there alone." She shivered. "Forget it. Let's catch a ride and go to the lake for a swim."

But Chloe felt something pulling her in the direction of the stones.

She wanted to take pictures and send a few to her granda. Ask him what he remembered.

"Hey, ladies. Lookin' good." A couple of guys visiting from New Jersey pulled over and rolled down the window. "Want to go for a swim with us?"

"Yes," Lola and Jules said at the same time.

"How about you, Chloe?" Benji leaned over to look out the open window. "Coming with us? Or you planning to sit in some boring garden and read all day?"

What a jerk. "I'm going to visit the stone circle."

Jules gasped. "Don't."

The boys laughed. "Oooh, isn't that the haunted place?" They made ghostly noises and tried to talk in scary voices, but only succeeded in sounding like they'd been watching too many B-movies.

Chloe rolled her eyes. "You guys have fun."

"Oh, come on. We're just teasing you," Benji said. "Get in. We'll drop you off on the way."

CHAPTER 5

THEY LET her off in Great Rollright. After wandering around the village and grabbing a bite to eat in a cute café with chintz dishes and window boxes full of flowers, Chloe found a place renting bicycles. They had a map that would guide her to the stones.

"If we're closed when you return, just lock up the bike," the owner, Ian, said. Then he tried to waggle his brows but only ended up looking like something had startled him. "Don't linger after dark. Wouldn't want you to disappear with the stones."

"Thanks, and ha ha. I'm sure it's fun to scare the tourists." It was only a couple of miles to the stone circle. The bike was red with a cute wicker basket on the front and a rack on the back. She'd purchased a couple bottles of water and an apple to bring with her.

Normally Chloe liked to read paperbacks or hardbacks. It was something about the smell of the paper, she guessed. But when she went on vacation, an e-reader was the only way she could bring enough books with her and not worry about lugging around fifty pounds of reading material.

She planned to ride around, spend some time taking pictures of the stones, and then spend the afternoon reading. Tonight she'd stay in town and catch a ride back to the hostel in the morning. Ian said he'd drive her after breakfast. It was the first day in a week it hadn't rained. The sky was a brilliant blue, a few lazy clouds floating by, and the sun reminded her of home. Closing her eyes, Chloe could almost smell the ocean, hear the waves crashing on the beach, and see Gull Cottage waiting to welcome her home, her grandparents on the porch enjoying a glass of wine before dinner.

Summers in Holden Beach were humid and hot, so sixty-five degrees almost felt a little chilly today. Biking in the sun would warm her up, so Chloe had worn a pair of jeans and a t-shirt that proclaimed, *I'm not antisocial, I'd just rather read.* A navy-blue hoodie went into her tote bag in case the temperature dropped this afternoon. Rain always made it feel cooler.

It was an effort, but she'd managed to pull her long curls into a ponytail and tie a navy ribbon around the pony holder to match her shirt. No flip-flops today. Chloe had left the beloved sparkly footwear she normally lived in back at the hostel, not knowing if she'd have to hike up to the circle or not. Instead, she'd worn a pair of white sneaker mules. They were comfortable and she could walk around all day. Mules were her favorite. Chloe hated the feeling of a shoe on her heel unless it was a boot. Weird, right? But oh well, that's who she was. The nice but kind of odd girl.

Tote bag secured on the bike rack, Chloe fished a pair of oversized dark sunglasses out of the tote, put them on, and pedaled out of town, enjoying the day.

The stones sat on a hill with spectacular views in all directions. Chloe parked the bike and twisted the cap off the water bottle, drinking deeply as the breeze brought the scent of freshly cut grass and another smell she'd come to recognize and love. The scent of old stone. It was a peaceful place with a kind of quiet energy. Like walking through Gettysburg or a very old cemetery. You lowered your voice, walked quietly, and were aware of all those who'd come before, the sacrifices they'd made for causes they believed in.

The stones were made of limestone and looked pitted, worn from the ravages of time. With nothing but time, she wandered among the stones, taking pictures with her phone. There was a metal railing around both the King Stone and the Whispering Knights so she couldn't get too close. Not that she wanted to—there was a feeling when she stood near the railing, telling her to go back, that she didn't belong in this place. With a nervous laugh, she moved away, looking over the landscape. The land was green, with tiny wildflowers growing amongst the stones.

Chloe had the place to herself as she walked around the King's Men stones. Birds sang and the sun warmed her skin. The three girls from Japan had said a witch turned a king and his knights to stone. And that the stones would disappear and reappear at odd times.

One of the locals told them there were so many stones, no one could ever count them correctly. The guy had leaned in close to them as he drank his pint. Most of the stories said if you could count the same number of stones three times, your heart's desire would come true.

His friend crossed himself and said no, that was wrong. The way he'd heard the tale was if you counted three times and got the same number of stones each time you counted, you would die a horrible death that very night.

The Australians laughed and said it was probably to keep people from damaging the stones. Then again, the girls lived with all kinds of poisonous snakes that could kill you in an instant, not to mention crocodiles. And while they said they didn't believe the stories, they weren't willing to risk any bad karma. That was how Chloe found herself alone with her thoughts with the entire day stretching out before her, all the time in the world to explore.

Hungry, she unhooked the tote bag from the back bike rack and picked a spot in the middle of the circle. There she spread her lunch out on an old tablecloth someone at the hostel had given her so she wouldn't get grass stains on her jeans.

Alone with her thoughts, she ate the hefty sandwich she'd bought from a pub in the village, enjoying the tang of the cheese and the crusty bread.

To have seen so many of the places her granda told her about made Chloe feel the history in every stone she touched, every street she

walked, and every building she passed. If only she were a "real" Merriweather.

Yes, she was by name, but not by blood. That was why nothing had
happened for her all these years. A cloud passed over the sun, and
Chloe shook her head.

"Stop it. You're eighteen and an adult." Okay, so maybe it was odd
that she spoke to herself out loud, but sometimes it helped her think,
to work through whatever issue she was struggling with. It wasn't like
there was anyone around to complain.

Lots of kids wanted to be astronauts or ballerinas or princesses or
dinosaurs, and they didn't go around for the next ten years acting all
sad because their childhood fantasy didn't come true. It was time to
forget silly childhood dreams and put away her fantasies of time
travel. Even though she knew time travel was possible. Her great-
aunts had traveled back in time, and Granda had come forward in
time. Ever since she could remember, she'd tried various experiments,
read everything she could on the matter, all to no avail.

Just because time travel happened for some people didn't mean it
would happen for her. Life wasn't fair, and it was time to get over it
and move on with her life. Figure out what she really wanted.

Chloe tidied up the remains of her lunch and went to pack it away
to take back to town and dispose of it there. Looking at the stones, she
squared her shoulders and glared. A sharp pain traveled from her
stomach to her heart as she made her decision.

"Fine. You win. I'll quit living in my head and join the real world."
And if she wiped a single tear away, it wasn't like there was anyone
around to notice.

She fastened the strap to keep the tote from blowing away. "Ow."
Chloe snatched her hand back, shaking it back and forth. Bright
droplets of blood landed on one of the stones. There must have been a
sharp edge on the bike rack.

The textured stone invited her to touch as she walked around the
circle, leaving little drops of blood on the stones. The air smelled of
green things growing, and a faint scent of roses helped wash away the

melancholy that sometimes filled her. Almost as if she had lived in another time and her soul yearned to go back.

A light breeze lifted the corner of the tablecloth. She straightened it out and lay down on her back, the crossbody bag under her head for a pillow. The bag of old coins she'd brought along at the last minute were lumpy, so she adjusted them until the bag was comfortable.

Too bad she didn't have a glass of Southern iced tea. Tea made everything better. Emotionally drained from the war within, she closed her eyes. The e-reader slid off her stomach and came to rest by her side. As Gram said, she'd just rest her eyes for a few minutes.

CHAPTER 6

"EDWIN," Richard bellowed as he hopped about on one foot.

"Yes, my lord?" His steward shuffled into the chamber, looking even more bent than the past summer. Nigh on two years Richard had been lord over Bainford, and in truth, he enjoyed the solitude. Richard snorted. Solitude.

"What is that infernal noise?" He'd sat on the trunk at the foot of the bed and examined the source of the pain. A wooden wolf with red on its snout seemed to mock him. How it ended up in his chamber was a mystery. One of the lads, no doubt.

Ever since a woodworker had come to Bainford seeking sanctuary, the small carvings had turned up in the strangest places. He'd found one in the garderobe, the stables, and a carved cat in the corner of the dungeon.

The man was a fourth son with no prospects, and as he did not wish to join the monastery, he entered the gates, asked to speak to Richard, and offered his skill in exchange for a bed and meals. In the man's favor, he did not flinch or cross himself—he met Richard's gaze, and when he accepted, the man fell to his knees, grateful. *Hrumph.*

Edwin took the carved wolf. "The lads offered Merry aid in catching the chickens. She is making chicken pie for supper."

"Mayhap I should ask," Richard said as he pulled on his boots. "Where were the chickens this time?"

The long-suffering sigh from his steward said what Richard had felt these past months. The castle had gone from a dozen souls to a score and three. Orphan children appeared as if left by the faeries. Some were left by their parents; others made their own way. The king could make good use of such knowledgeable spies.

How did they know to come to Bainford? When asked, Richard heard the same answer: they heard on the road or in the tavern or on the streets.

"Never mind. 'Tis better I do not know. I'll sort them out."

"As you say, my lord." Edwin shuffled across the floor. "One was in your solar, sitting on the stool before the fire."

Richard covered his ears. "Nay, do not tell me more." Blasted chickens. He ignored the state of his hall as he strode outside. The walls were bare, the decayed paneling ripped down and removed by the Irish, the furniture was sparse, and the table coverings all chewed by vermin. Then again, his coffers, cellar, and larder were full and his tunics clean. Outside, the sun warmed his bones. Mayhap this was the best life he could hope for.

The Irishmen finished repairs to the chapel and garrison. Next they would see to his hall. The outer walls would withstand any attack, the moat was full of fish, and the drawbridge was new and sturdy. The past two years had been filled with much-needed work, and if Richard caught sight of his ruined visage, he simply looked away. There were enough children at Bainford; he had no need of a wife and could seek out a wench if needs be. If he kept telling himself, perchance he would believe it to be so.

A carriage accompanied by five riders rolled into the courtyard, and he found himself besieged on all sides.

"I see the walls are in good repair, though you've need of more men to guard the place." Garrick dismounted, brushing the dust from his hose.

The door to the carriage opened, and two women stepped out,

followed by two children. Mouth slack, Richard watched. Saints, not more of the imps.

"Richard, I have brought you two chairs. Garrick says you've nowhere to sit in this decrepit hall of yours."

"Edith. You traveled all the way from London in this weather? Is your husband vexing you again?" Richard embraced Garrick's eldest sister. "Where are the rest of your fetching sisters?"

She sniffed. "Busy having babes and running their households. Margery is still unwed, if you have decided to marry."

Richard looked to Garrick, who backed away, holding his hands out. "I want no part of womanly schemes." He grinned over his shoulder. "I'm for the lists. If you're wise, you'll join me anon."

Richard proffered his arm to Edith, careful to keep her on his left so she would not suffer to look upon him.

"Shall I run your husband through? You always wanted to visit distant lands."

She patted his arm. "Nay. I will poison him if he becomes troublesome."

"Mistress?" The serving woman stayed close to the carriage.

"Come along," Edith said.

The woman crossed herself. "Nay, I cannot. The beast will kill me and eat the children."

Richard knew that look of displeasure on her face. He stepped back, for there was no stopping Edith when she was in a temper.

"You will take the children to the kitchens and wait for me there. I will have no talk of beasts. Lord Bainford saved my brother's life. Say another word and I will see you beaten."

Wetness leaking down her face, the girl nodded. "Yes, mistress."

"Tales of the black keep with its demon have spread to London." Edith rolled her eyes. "I see you find this most pleasing. I brought gifts."

"Aye. I see the gifts quite well with my one eye." Richard snorted. The chairs were but a bribe for him to take in two more children.

The girl hid behind the servant while her brother darted looks at him. The boys were terrified and fascinated at the same time. Richard scowled and hid a grin when the boy ducked behind the servant's skirts.

He saw Edith settled in one of the new chairs before the fire then sent the servants for wine.

"In truth, you will always find sanctuary here," Richard said. "I will not let your husband use you ill."

Edith stretched her toes before the fire. "Everand does not beat me. He is too busy with his mistress." She patted his hand. "Do not worry overmuch; my sisters live close by and are fine company. I have two children and a home. It is enough."

Edith was the eldest, then Garrick. There were six other sisters: Meg, Ella, Beatrice, Beverly, Heloise, and little Margery.

"Has Margery any prospects for suitors?" Garrick had wished for Richard to wed the girl, but he refused. 'Twas enough to see the loathing on the merchants' faces. He would not bear such from a wife. Nay, he would rather be alone.

"The blacksmith will offer for her. It is a good match." Edith accepted the goblet of wine from the servant. They sat in silence while Richard waited for her to tell him the reason for her visit.

Edith cleared her throat. "You know what is being said about you in London?"

"I can guess." Richard looked at his blue tunic and hose. Both had been mended many times. 'Twas time to send for the merchant for more cloth. His men and the children also required new clothing, so he would see it done as much as it pained him.

"Can you?" Cool gray eyes met his.

She was plain, yet he found her eyes reminded him of a winter sky, and the kindness he saw within made her beautiful.

"No one willingly ventures here," she continued. "You cannot keep men nor servants; they run shrieking from your hall. Why do you encourage these rumors? There are tales of parents leaving their changeling children at the gates of Bainford for the beast to eat. Others tell of tying up orphans and leaving them as sacrifices to the beast to ensure a good harvest."

"Superstitions. You know 'tis not true."

"Aye. But men are foolish, and I do not wish to hear my brother was killed fighting a mob come to drive away the devil."

"I wish to be left alone. Garrick is free to go where he pleases." Richard drained his wine.

Edith looked at his hall, her nose wrinkled at the dirty rushes on the floor and bare walls. He had been busy with the outer defenses these past years. There were no longer holes in his roof—the rest of the hall could wait.

"Garrick is loyal." She cocked her head. "As are you. To a fault." Edith placed a hand on his arm. "There is one truth in the rumors. I see the children."

"I will not turn them away."

"Nay, I know this, Richard," she said softly. "'Tis why I brought the boy and the girl."

"There was nowhere for them in London?"

Her gray dress swept the floor as she took his arm and walked with him around the hall.

"Their parents died. I was buying cloth when I saw them. They had been caught stealing bread. You know what happens to orphan children. I could not leave them, and Everand would not feed beggars." She held up a hand. "I do not want your gold—we have enough, but not enough to feed any more mouths."

Edith frowned as two dogs ran through the hall chased by two boys, shrieking like the very hounds of hell Richard was oft compared to.

She sighed, hands on her hips. "Wade has seven years and Maron five. The children need a home and you need servants. The boy can work in the stables, the girl in the gardens—what is left of them."

Richard knew when he was bested. "I will see to them."

She nodded and looked away, rubbing her eyes, but not before Richard saw her leaking. He might have rolled his eye had he not found a speck of dust preventing him from doing such.

In the morn, after a bout in the lists with Garrick, Richard saw Edith off then went in search of the children. He found them staring into the moat.

Crouching beside them, he peered into the dark water. "What do you see?"

The girl jumped. But the boy pointed. "Fish."

"Aye. There are some big ones swimming in there. Good eating." Richard eyed the urchin. "Do ye fish?"

"I cannot swim. How do I catch them?" His clothes were tattered and stained. The way he scratched told Richard the boy would have to bathe or spread lice to all the children.

"Robin will show you." He looked to the girl. She was sitting still as if she might escape his notice if she did not move.

"Maron. Why did you and your brother steal?" Richard kept his gaze on the water, not wanting to startle the child. Edwin was fond of telling him he bellowed like the giants of old.

She was dirty, her hair matted, yet he could see a smile under the hair she kept over her face.

"We tried to work but none would have us. And we was hungry."

"Our parents died of a sickness," the boy said. "Then we had no place to live, so we slept in old buildings." He met Richard's gaze but did not flinch at what he saw. "I kept Maron safe. She is my responsibility."

Richard respected that. "You will not steal from me."

"Nay, my lord," they said.

"If you do, I will eat you."

The boy jumped, and Richard grinned. "Nay, methinks you would not have enough meat on you to feed the beast." Then he struck true fear into their little hearts. "If you wish to live here at Bainford, you will have a bath and clean clothes."

The children looked stricken. They whispered, then Wade and his sister stood, shoulder to shoulder.

"We will bathe, my lord."

"Go find Merry. She will give you new clothes." Richard stood, his leg sore from crouching so long. "After, you will have a proper meal."

It seemed Bainford had become the home of lost souls, damaged men, and orphans.

CHAPTER 7

So cold. Wait. Why was it freezing cold? Groggy and disoriented, Chloe woke fully to find she'd wrapped the tablecloth around her and was shivering. Something wet hit her face.

"What the heck?"

It was snowing. It didn't snow in England in July.

"No, no, no." She stumbled over to where she'd left her bike, only to find someone had happened by and stolen it while she was sleeping.

Chloe pulled the blanket tighter, walking around where she'd sworn she'd left the bike. There were no footprints or tire tracks. How long had it been snowing? "Long enough to cover the thief's tracks, obviously."

Even worse, the unknown person had taken her e-reader and phone, too. No reading material and no way to call and check in with her family. Her mom was going to be furious by the time Chloe made it back to town, reported the bike missing, and replaced the electronics. At least everything was stored in the cloud so she hadn't lost anything other than the devices, which were expensive enough, but she was trying to look on the bright side, thank you very much.

Thank the stars the crossbody bag containing her money and passport hadn't been stolen. Likely because she'd used it as a pillow. Nearby trees offered shelter from the fat, fluffy snowflakes as she leaned against a wide trunk and then slid down to sit on a fallen tree and take stock of the situation.

"Time to see what you do have."

She emptied the crossbody bag at her feet, grateful she hadn't worn flip-flops. Flip-flops in the snow. A half-hysterical laugh escaped before she clapped a hand over her mouth. Some kind of humming noise emanating off the stones made her want to be quiet.

Let's see. She had her passport, money, lip balm, and the bag of coins from Granda. There were a couple of ponytail holders, a candy bar, and a small box of matches she'd gotten from a pub because she liked the logo.

From town to the stones was a couple of miles. No one had passed by when she'd ridden to the stones, nor the entire time she'd been there, so it was not likely she'd luck out and catch a ride. Chloe could hear her mom's voice screaming that she was going to be murdered hitchhiking, but Chloe figured it was more likely she'd be picked up by a little old lady who fed her biscuits and tea and showed her a million pictures of her grandkids or little toy dogs.

"Suck it up, buttercup," Chloe muttered as she traipsed through the snow, her feet wet and freezing from the slush filling her shoes. Why hadn't she splurged and bought the pair of bright pink Hunter rain boots like she'd seen girls on the street wearing, instead of going with her comfortable sneaker mules?

Without her phone, Chloe didn't know how much time had passed, only that her teeth were chattering, she couldn't feel her toes, and there was no sign of the road. How had the snow gotten so deep so fast? It had to be a freak storm. Tomorrow the sun would come out, it would be in the low seventies, and this would all be a distant memory.

Onward she trudged, until Chloe had to admit the facts. She had no coat, impractical shoes, and was completely lost.

The pale sun sat low in the sky when she finally came to some sort of sketchy-looking pub. Talk about rustic. But the smell of freshly baked bread and some kind of soup or stew made her mouth water. When she pushed the door open, she stopped, blinking, her mouth open, trying to take in what her eyes were seeing, but her mind was refusing to comprehend.

"Hell's bells," she muttered, using one of her gram's favorite expressions. It was smoky inside, but at least it was warm, with a roaring fire going in the fireplace. Smells assaulted her nose. The good smells of bread and stew mixed with the smell of old beer and body odor, and she sniffed again. Wet dog. Yuck.

"Don't stand there gaping." A girl about her age stood in front of Chloe, dressed in a long dress with a dirty apron over it.

"I get it. This is one of those tourist places." Relief filled Chloe once she'd made sense of the oddly dressed patrons. The waitress led her over to a small table tucked into the corner by the fire.

"Lost your coat, did ye?" The girl looked Chloe up and down, frowning. "'Tis an odd cloak. I've never seen the like. I'll fetch you a cup of ale and a nice bowl of stew." She bustled away, leaving Chloe to warm her frozen bits and take in the surroundings.

The roof was thatched, and the walls had what looked like mud and straw holding them together, with a few spots where the cold air whistled in through the chinks. There were rough tables and benches placed haphazardly about, with a few tiny tables tucked into the corners of the room.

Everyone looked so authentic. The men wore rough peasant garb, with a few wearing tunics and hose, while the women wore simple dresses. There hadn't been any mention of this place in the information Chloe had read about the town. She must have been so excited to see the stones that she'd completely missed it. Wait until she told Jules and Lola. They'd love this place…though maybe not the smell.

The waitress came back with a wooden bowl filled with a savory vegetable stew, a chunk of brown bread, and a cup of ale. Starved, Chloe dug in. Fascinated by the tableau in front of her, she bit down on the bread and winced.

It was a tiny pebble. So that was a little too authentic for her tastes. She placed it on the table and took another bite, only to find more pebbles.

This time, she looked closely at the patrons, unease bubbling up within her. The waitress came by and refilled her cup.

"Can you believe this snow? It was sunny and warm this morning."

The girl took a step back. "Been snowing for a se'nnight, mistress. And colder this winter than last."

Chloe put the spoon down. "Pardon? Did you say winter?"

The girl gave her a look like she was totally clueless. "Aye. Winter."

"Um…if you don't mind me asking. What month is it?"

The girl crossed herself. "The first day of November, mistress." And she scurried away, whispering to another server.

"November." Chloe snorted. That was funny. It was July. Summer, not winter. Was she dreaming?

Careful to keep the tablecloth wrapped around her, she reached up and pinched the underside of her arm.

"Ouch. Okay, then. Not hallucinating." Thank goodness the tan tablecloth looked enough like linen that she fit in, at least while sitting. It dragged on the ground too, so no one could see her shoes. A funny feeling swirled through her, but before she could give voice to the thoughts, the door banged open and three men stumbled in. They looked rough, typical ruffians come to create mayhem for the guests. Chloe wondered where the restaurant had found them.

No one broke character. So either this was like Disney, where the workers had to stay in character no matter what, or they were filming one of those reality shows where people lived like they did in the past to see if they could make a go of it. There had been a Victorian show she'd remembered a while back that was similar.

Trying not to call attention to herself and mess up the filming, Chloe looked for the cameras. As she was wondering if the people were wearing cameras as well, a snippet of conversation had her leaning toward the sound to hear the patrons at the table next to her. It was something about their tone that had caught her attention.

There were three waitresses huddled together by the wall, talking in low voices.

"Aye, my sister went to work for the beast and never returned."

"Beast?" Chloe said. "I'm sorry. I didn't mean to eavesdrop, but is there an escaped animal running around?"

The girl with a long red braid put her hands on her hips, looked around the room, and then nodded. All three of them huddled around Chloe's table.

"Aye. You talk strangely. Where are you from, mistress?"

The waitress with black hair said, "And where is your escort?"

"I'm traveling for the sum—for the year," Chloe said. Deciding to play along, she added, "My husband is seeing to our horses." That seemed to do the trick. The serving girl refilled the cup again, and Chloe hoped she wouldn't be drunk by the time she left. "You were talking about a beast. Will you tell me?"

She recognized the signs of a good gossip fest as the three girls looked around to make sure they weren't overheard and that no one was calling for them. Then the redhead, who seemed to be the leader, said, "'Twas the deepest of nights when the beast appeared at Bainford Castle."

The raven-haired girl crossed herself. "Aye. The devil himself sent him. The beast is deformed. He wears a black cloth over one eye." She leaned closer. "'Tis said if you look under the cloth, the eye glows red with hellfire."

The three girls told Chloe story after story of the beast, and the room filled with unease as thick as the smoke from the fire as the girls spun their tales.

"No one will set foot near the castle. The ones who did never returned," the dark-haired server said.

The redhead, eyes round, whispered, "I heard he ate them."

Willing herself not to laugh, Chloe pressed her lips together.

The dark-haired girl put a hand to her chest. "The Beast of Bainford never leaves the castle. He is cursed by the devil to walk the grounds of Bainford until his master drags him back to hell."

The redhead nodded. "If you look upon his face, he will ensnare you to do his unholy bidding."

The door banged open and all four of them jumped, knocking the ale over. It ran across the table and dripped onto the floor, looking a bit like blood on the dirty stone.

CHAPTER 8

RICHARD YAWNED, resting his elbows on the table, nodding into his trencher. Merry was a good cook; the bread did not have pebbles in it and the fish was crisp. He poked at a mess of green, not liking the taste, but he shoveled the weeds into his mouth and chewed quickly, not wishing to hurt the girl's feelings.

The children were convinced there was a ghost wandering about Bainford. For the past fortnight they had run shrieking from their beds at night into his chamber, piling in his bed like a litter of puppies. The men had found nothing amiss. Richard had not heard the wailing, but the children swore 'twas a fearsome noise.

A se'nnight passed and still children woke screaming in the night. Richard swore he would banish the ghost. That eve, he was in the hall, staring into the fire, listening to the snores of the servants bedded down against the hearth, when he heard it. The wail was faint, coming from somewhere in the castle. The sword hissed as he pulled it from the scabbard and went in search of spirits.

The sound of snoring came from the garrison as he walked the grounds.

"Have you heard any odd noises?" he called to the guard on the wall.

The man scratched his beard. "Nay, my lord. 'Tis the wind, nothing more."

Hrumph. Richard walked through the chapel, peering into the corners, though he did not believe a ghost would haunt a holy place, unless 'twas a priest who thought he was not dead. The stables were quiet, the horses calm; the stable boys were asleep in the hay. Convinced the sound was coming from inside the castle, he heard it again as he passed by his solar.

There was a passageway leading to the top of the east tower that was rarely used. The other towers required repair before they would be safe enough. Sword at the ready, Richard climbed the stairs, shadows appearing on the wall, and the wailing grew louder.

He pushed the wooden door open to see the newest arrival to the castle, little Maron, curled up in a ball before the cold hearth, a candle flickering. She was weeping, the sound piercing his heart like the arrow that took his eye.

Not wanting to startle her, Richard slid down the wall to sit next to her and said softly, "Tell me what ails you, child."

Impossibly blue eyes full of tears looked up at him. The child threw herself into his arms and wailed. Not sure what to do, Richard awkwardly patted her on the back, murmuring soft words, as he did when caring for his horses or hounds.

When he shifted to ease the pain in his leg, she sniffed and blew her nose on his tunic.

"Has someone hurt you? I will run them through, lass."

Maron wiped her face, sniffling. "I miss my mama. It's so quiet here, not 'tall like London, and it scares me something fierce."

She was a tiny thing, curled up in his lap and clutching his tunic. "Why are you up here, alone in the cold and the dark?"

With her long, curly black hair and those wise eyes, she looked like a tiny faerie. "I didn't want Robin to hear me weeping. He says we must be strong or you will send us away and we will starve and die." The weeping continued.

Her little shoulders were thin under the wool of her green dress. Richard tilted her chin up.

"Hear me well, lass. Bainford is your home. I will never send you away. You and your brother may live here the rest of your lives if you so desire. The larder is full; you will not starve." He patted her back, almost sending her sprawling. "In time you will die—death comes to us all. But not today, and if the fates smile upon us, you will not die until you are older than Edwin."

"You are a good man, my lord." She wrinkled her nose, tapping a finger against her lips. "How do I stop missing my mama?"

He blew out a breath. "You will always miss her. When someone we love dies, their absence leaves a wound that never heals. In time, it will leave a scar and no longer hurt as you are being cleaved in two. Your mama is always with you."

"How is she with me? I can't see her." Maron curled up like a kitten and wiped her nose on his other sleeve.

"Nay, you cannot see her—she has gone to the beyond. But her love for you will always be in your heart. Talk to Robin about her, tell each other what you remember, and you will keep her with you always."

"I want to be strong like you." She wound a curl around her finger.

"You are as strong as a warrior, little one. Now, no more weeping at night. You're scaring everyone. They think there is a ghost at Bainford."

"I told them there was no ghost," she scoffed. "They are witless dolts." She sounded just like him. Richard pressed his lips together so he would not laugh.

"I am sorry I scared them." She blinked up at him. "The villagers are scared of you, but I am not. I told them Lord Bainford is not a beast, but I don't think they believed me."

Maron mumbled something he could not make out, yawned, and fell asleep, her tiny hand in his.

Richard did not know how long he sat holding her close, looking at her tiny fingers.

"My lord?" Edwin peered into the room, holding a candle.

Richard held a finger to his lips and whispered, "Do not wake the child."

His steward took the child as Richard got to his feet, wincing from sitting so long.

"I will carry her." Richard took the sleeping child, carried her to the chamber where the girls slept in a large bed, and covered her with a blanket.

As he stood there, looking at the children, an odd feeling filled him. Mayhap these unwanted children would be his family. He did not need a wife. It did not matter he wished for a woman to love him. To not care he was a bastard with a ruined face. He shut the door behind him.

Nay, 'twas a childish dream. Wishes were for children.

CHAPTER 9

"My LORD, if you but hold still," Edwin said.

Richard cursed fluently. "How long, man?" he bellowed at the merchant cowering at his feet. Anything to cover his shaking leg. If he did not soon sit, his leg would give way and Richard would not fall on his face in front of this paltry man.

"Truly, I am sorry, my lord." The man scurried about to finish his measurements.

"When you finish, see to tunics and hose for the men and boys. And gowns for the women and girls."

"As you wish, my lord."

"Nothing too costly. We labor at Bainford."

"Of course, my lord." The man nodded and pulled out plain woolens in gray, brown, and greens.

The man had implored Richard to wear a more fashionable tunic, with the sleeves wide enough that he would trip. How could a man fight when he could not see his bloody sword? The merchant draped blue silk across Richard.

"At court, my lord—"

"I care naught for court. Bloody hell, do I look like a courtier to you, man?"

The man gulped. "Nay, my lord." His hand shaking, he finished and scurried from the solar.

❦

THE TAVERN OWNER called to the servers to quit talking and get back to work, breaking up the gossip. Chloe gave the establishment credit: they'd done a great job on making the place look authentic. The dirt on the floors was a bit too authentic, but she was out in the middle of nowhere.

The outlandish stories the girls told her about the beast were so over the top that Chloe could almost see a pair of red glowing eyes in the dimly lit corner of the tavern. She rubbed her arms. Obviously, the scary stories were a ploy to get people to pay to visit the nearby castle. Someone was good at marketing. They knew their customers. Chloe was definitely going there next. After those stories? She had to see the place for herself. "Excuse me, miss? How much do I owe you?"

The woman told her an amount, but it didn't sound right. To be on the safe side, Chloe handed her a credit card.

The girl frowned. "What is this?" She turned the card over and over, smelled it, and then bit the corner. She made a face and handed it back to Chloe.

Guess they only took cash. Chloe handed over a twenty-pound note and the same routine ensued. Was she supposed to have exchanged her money for whatever they used here before ordering? Inspiration struck when she noticed a few of the old coins her granda had given her had fallen out of the crossbody bag and were lying on the table. The drawstrings on the pouch must have come loose.

The server picked out a couple of the coins and laid the twenty on the table. "Best keep yer fortune hidden." She nodded at the patrons. "There are those here would slit yer throat for what you have."

Well, that was a bit more realistic than Chloe wanted. "Do you have a room? It's too late to go back to the village."

The girl held out a hand again, and, not sure how much to give her, Chloe fished out a handful of coins and let the girl take a few. She hoped the antique coins weren't too valuable, or she'd feel awful for wasting them on a simple meal and a room.

"Come along." Without waiting for a response, the girl led Chloe up a set of rickety stairs. They passed two doors before the girl opened the final door at the end of the hall. The room was rustic, the bed looked lumpy, and Chloe had never been so happy.

"I will see to the fire, mistress." The girl bustled around the room, built up the fire, and turned to go.

"Is there someplace I can wash up?" Chloe asked. The girl pointed to a basin and ewer on a wooden board attached to the wall.

She paused in the doorway. "Bolt the door. Unless ye want company tonight."

"Thanks." Chloe hurried over and threw the simple latch, hoping the door was sturdy. Though surely the restaurant-slash-inn wouldn't take things so far as to make the guests feel unsafe?

No toothbrush or other toiletries in sight—not to mention a bathroom. She used a finger to scrub her teeth as best she could. Mud spattered the tablecloth and her clothes, so they had to go. No way was she sleeping in dirty clothes.

At least there was what looked like a linen washcloth and a small lump of awful-smelling soap. Once undressed, she washed as best she could. The rag did a decent job of getting rid of the worst of the mud from her jeans and shoes. There was an iron stand near the fire, so she put everything there to dry and wrapped herself up in the tablecloth. The bright pink undies and bra looked funny in the old-fashioned room. A small stool by the fire beckoned her to sit and warm herself. Grateful and clean, Chloe nodded off.

The feeling of falling startled her awake as she landed on her butt next to the stool in an unfamiliar room.

Blinking, she saw her clothes on the stand. "Right. The pub." Chloe checked the clothes to find they were dry.

"No. You have got to be kidding me." So that was what the smell was: a charred scrap of pink lay half out of the fire, and as she reached for it, it caught fire and was no more. The silky material of the bra and undies must have caused them to slip off the stand and into the fire.

She put on her t-shirt, thankful it came down over her bum, and left the jeans by the bed. With the last of the water, she washed the tablecloth and hung it to dry.

Exhausted, she climbed into the lumpy bed, refusing to think about bedbugs.

§.

"LEAVE ME ALONE," Chloe mumbled, and burrowed deeper into the bed.

A rough hand on her bare hip jolted her awake. "Get off me," she yelled, and elbowed the body next to her.

There was a man in her room. In her bed. She'd been so careful at the hostels to keep her valuables safe and watch out for creeps. All the girls watched out for each other. How had he gotten in her room?

It must have been when she'd gotten up to find a bathroom in the night. There was no sink, only a hole in the floor with cold air coming up. She'd never taken care of business and ran so fast in her life, once she'd checked that no one was in the hall. All she could think was that she'd hadn't latched the door properly, she'd been so tired and disoriented.

"Hey, I said no."

The man was heavy and only grunted before pawing at her again, so she did what she had to and kneed him. Hard. The man yelped and rolled off her.

In that moment, Chloe grabbed the sheet to wrap around her and leaped out of bed. But she wasn't fast enough. The man jumped up so quickly that she never saw it coming as he punched her in the stomach. The air left her with a whoosh, and she fell back, desperately sucking in air, tears running into her hair. The pain was intense. She couldn't breathe. Panic set in as the man leered at her.

Liquid fear replaced the blood in her veins as she saw the intent on the man's face. There was realistic and then there was completely and utterly wrong.

"Ye may be addled in the head, but yer body is fine, wench. I will enjoy your favors and then give you to my men."

He sat on her. The tiny bit of breath she'd managed to suck in whooshed out, and Chloe desperately tried to buck him off, which only served to make the creep laugh.

The alcoholic fumes coming off him were enough to set her eyes watering. He had on some kind of ridiculous top with the most enormous sleeves she'd ever seen. You could fit a small car in those sleeves.

Sucking in a bit of air, Chloe fisted the excess fabric in both hands and yanked as hard as she could. His drunkenness was what saved her, as he lost his balance and went tumbling off her.

A yelp escaped as she kicked him in the stomach and her bare foot connected with some kind of metal. She snatched her bag, shoes, and jeans from the floor. Then she ran for the door, hurdling the drunk like she was first in line at a Lilly Pulitzer sample sale.

He made a grab for her and got hold of the sheet, and she had no choice but to let it go. Ignoring the fact she was running downstairs clad in nothing more than a t-shirt, Chloe sprinted for the door.

There were people sleeping on the floor. She hurdled them, yanked the door open, and escaped into...a winter wonderland.

"What's with all the snow? It's supposed to be July, not November." Why would a restaurant haul in snow? Was it some kind of festival? It had to have cost a fortune.

A small, sleepy-looking boy carrying a bucket of water in each hand stared at her, mouth open in the early morning light. Chloe looked at the bundle in her arms. Somehow she'd grabbed the guy's coat along with her stuff. Grateful she had something warm, she yanked her jeans on, slid her feet into her sneakers, and wrapped what looked like some type of long cloak around her, making sure to hide the crossbody bag under the coat.

With a wave to the boy, she walked as fast as she could through the snow into the woods. She'd go to the castle the waitstaff had talked about last night. Who cared if the place was supposed to be haunted?

It had to be better than being here and risking another assault. The castle would have a phone. She could call someone to take her back to the hostel and then call her family. A small voice told her perhaps she might not find a phone there. Or anywhere, for that matter.

"Shut up," she told the voice, and focused on getting away before the creep decided to come after her.

What did it say about how rattled she was that Chloe was willing to face the Beast of Bainford and beg for sanctuary?

CHAPTER 10

UNABLE TO SLEEP, Richard paced the battlements. It had snowed last night, turning everything white. When he was tired of pacing, he walked about gazing at the repairs that had been made these past three years. The men had done well. His home would soon be a fortress.

His fearsome black reputation had men eager to stand before the gates of Bainford. They paid dearly in gold to cross swords with the beast. To best him. In the time he had spent here, isolated from others, Richard had amassed a large amount of hard-won gold. Enough to stock his larder and fund all necessary repairs and many improvements. None but the Irish would stay. Other men came but left within a day, swearing his home was haunted. The cowards told tales in the villages of how they had survived after seeing the beast, black as night, running through the forests, eyes red and glowing with the fires of hell. Dolts. The lot of them. With each tale, his reputation grew until Richard himself was impressed.

He had a new blacksmith, a giant of a man who told Richard he knew he was going to hell, so he would gladly keep company with the beast.

In the stables, Richard went to his horse, a great black stallion with a spot of white on his face.

"Shall we ride?" The horse nickered as Richard saddled him. He preferred to saddle his own mount—treachery in the king's army had taught him well. The cloak and hood in place, he rode through the gates, only to see a lump cowering in the mud.

"Please, my lord. Don't eat me."

"By the saints." Richard scowled at the pile of rags. The boy was puny, with bright red hair.

Richard dismounted, cursing wholeheartedly. The sound of riders approaching had him reaching for his sword.

"More offerings to the beast?" Garrick pointed at the boy cowering against the stone wall.

Grumbling, Richard stomped about for a bit. "You, boy." The child yelped and crouched down, covering his head with his scrawny arms.

"Don't scare the lad." Garrick hauled the boy up. "Who brought you to Bainford?"

The boy swallowed a few times before getting the words out. "No one. I walked."

"Walked? From where?" Richard frowned.

"Cornwall," the boy squeaked.

Richard gaped at the boy. "Alone?"

The child nodded. "My da sold me to pay his debts. The man said I was no good to him, and he left me by the sea. Along the way I heard about the b—about Bainford."

Garrick grinned at Richard. "And you came to face the beast? Were you not afraid?"

The boy trembled. "Aye. But I've nowhere else to go. Thought I might get a meal before the beast dragged me to hell." He squinted at Richard. "You don't look like a beast. My da had burns on his face like you. Got them when my uncle pushed him in the fire." He looked through the tunnel. "Does the monster wander about during the day?"

"Cease," Richard said. "Garrick, see the child to the kitchens.

Merry will tell him what he needs do if he wishes to stay at Bainford."

𝕱

CHLOE RAN where the snow had been packed down like some sort of path, and walked or stumbled when it was too deep to run. Back home in Holden Beach, she'd have been curled up at Gram's, drinking hot chocolate and watching the snow fall on the ocean. They didn't get much snow, so whenever they did, it was a major event.

Between the numbness in her feet and the stitch in her side, Chloe knew she couldn't keep up this pace for much longer. Gritting her teeth, she pressed a hand to her side and slogged onward, hoping the castle would appear soon.

Sometime later, nature called and she needed to rest. Chloe found a spot in some bushes and took care of business. Leaning against a tree, sucking in deep breaths, she almost missed the noise over the sound of her heart thumping in her ears. She hadn't seen a road or single car or power line. The reality of the situation kept bouncing around in her head, but she kept pushing it away, not sure if she wanted it to be real or not. After all, some things sounded wonderful in theory, but in reality weren't so great. Yes, it was the sound of horses.

"Nutella on toast." Chloe was tired, sore, and grouchy. Not to mention hungry, since she'd run out of the pub without breakfast. Three men on horses rode into the clearing. Afraid they would spot her, Chloe dropped to her knees and crawled into the brush—not the bushes where she'd done her business, because that would be gross, but a huge clump of thick bushes with a natural or animal-made opening near the bottom. Using her elbows, she wriggled forward on her stomach until she could see through a gap. The clean smell of the forest and the snow cleared out her sinuses. It was starting to get to her that she hadn't heard any planes or seen the contrails in the sky.

Thank goodness none of the men looked like that drunk creep from the pub. These men were dressed similarly to the men last night, though maybe a bit nicer—the fabric looked better quality. Something shiny caught her eye. Each of them had a knife or small sword hanging on their hip. Either the whole area was a big "welcome to the past" exhibit or she had done the one thing she'd dreamed about since she was a little girl.

It was hard not to yell. She felt both excitement at having made it to the past and sorrow. Because if she truly had traveled through time and not just wandered into some kind of playground for history buffs, she might not see her family ever again.

Chloe chewed on her lip. *She* hadn't done anything but fall asleep. Somehow, the stones had sent her back in time. But to when? Based on what she'd seen, maybe the Middle Ages? But that was a lot of years, and some of them terrible. *No, don't get your hopes up yet. Make sure you really did it. The countryside of England could look the same now as hundreds of years ago, so until you know, no getting all giddy.*

As she watched the men, trying to decide whether or not to come out and ask for help, one of them snarled at the other. There was an air of danger about the men, something about their demeanor. She'd been in a bad part of Durham one weekend with friends and they'd passed three guys on the street. No one said anything, but they all crossed the street and went into the first busy café she and her friends could find.

The men hadn't done anything; it was more like an aura around them that she and her friends could see, telling them the men were trouble. These men had the same look. They certainly weren't the chivalrous knights her granda had told her about. No, these guys would rob her, defile her, and slit her throat. Then use her body for a couch and eat their lunch. So she stayed hidden, watching, looking for clues as the day passed.

Cold and wet, Chloe decided the men were loud enough that they wouldn't hear her moving in the brush. It was getting late in the day and she wanted to find the castle and ask for shelter before dark. Otherwise, being wet and without proper shoes or gloves, she'd freeze out here in the snow.

Hopefully she could buy food and a room for the night. *Thank you, Granda, for the antique coins*—or should she say modern-day coins?

Because if she was right, her paper pound notes were now worthless, good only for kindling or toilet paper.

The sound of horses and voices made her freeze in place, half in and half out of the brush. Two men rode into the clearing and all hell broke loose.

The juxtaposition between the pretty falling snow and the clanging of swords was surreal. Chloe clapped a hand to her mouth to keep from screaming when one of the men fell to the ground a few inches from her face. Open, unseeing eyes looked through her as the snow turned red beneath him.

At that moment, Chloe was completely sure of three things:

1. The man in front of her was dead.

2. She had indeed traveled through time, and the bloodthirsty, violent stories her granda told her were not embellished.

3. Time travel was fun in theory but not so much in reality.

Chloe had always thought it would be so much fun to travel back in time and meet the Merriweather women she'd heard so much about. Have a few laughs, clear up some questions about things she'd always wondered about, and then go home. In her daydreams, she always came back home to her family. What was life without a family to anchor you in the world?

Since she had no idea *how* she'd traveled through time or how the stones worked—Granda had told her, but even he wasn't really sure— Chloe would need every molecule of brainpower to blend in.

First, she'd find out *when* she was. Then she would use her money to hire a guide to escort her to Falconburg Castle, because she knew it wasn't safe for a woman to travel alone. Once she'd arrived, she would ask to see Melinda Merriweather, introduce herself, spend a week or two there, and then go back to the stones and go home.

Elation to worry and back again in a big circle. Chloe's emotions were all over the place. Elation because she was here in the past. Somewhere in medieval England. Worry because her mom, Arthur, and her grandparents would be worried they hadn't heard from her. And when they couldn't reach her on the phone? Not knowing what had happened to her? Would they figure out she'd traveled through time? More likely, they would think she had died just like Lucy Merri-weather's sisters had thought about her before they too traveled through time.

It wasn't like Chloe could buy a ticket on a boat and go to America. She was hundreds of years away from everyone she loved. They hadn't even been born yet. Well, Granda had. He had left the past in 1335. Wouldn't it be funny if she ran into him? It was imperative she find out the year. Why hadn't she asked the serving girl? At least Chloe knew it was the second of November. Weird how it was July in her time and winter now.

Thoughts flitted through her mind like fireflies on a hot summer night at the beach as she stayed still in the snow, wet and shivering. If she somehow managed to find Melinda, just wait until Chloe told her all about her granda. Her gram had told Chloe she'd never told her sister or nieces about Drake. Wouldn't they be surprised?

"You there."

A hand reached through and snatched Chloe's hand. With a gasp, she scrabbled backward, striking the man's hand with her other fist. When he didn't let go, she grabbed hold of a branch, pulled it back as far as she could, and let it go. It smacked the man in the face. Snow fell on his head, and that was all the time she needed to escape.

Once again, Chloe found herself running from horrible men through the woods and snow. The men called after her, yelling to each other. The snow muffled the sounds; the crunch of the snow and her breathing was loud in her ears as she willed her legs to move faster.

They were gaining on her, close enough she could smell onion and body odor. Hoping it would help, Chloe breathed through her mouth and prayed. She burst out of the woods into a clearing. Ahead of her loomed a castle so stark and forbidding that it had to be Bainford, the one the girls told her about.

Digging deep within, she pushed harder than she ever had, willing her feet to go faster and make it to the castle in time. She only hoped the men inside were nicer than the ones chasing her. If anybody up there was listening, it would also be nice if the beast didn't kill her on the spot.

CHAPTER 11

RICHARD SPENT THE DAY RIDING. He did not care overmuch for the dark of winter, the lack of sunlight. It made him disagreeable. 'Twas almost time for supper. His horse, wanting his own meal, turned for home when a cat ran in front of them, a small creature struggling in its jaws. Not only was Richard's hall overrun with children, but now hounds and cats.

He blamed Maron. One morn she found him in his solar and told him why there needs be cats at Bainford. The villagers would say the devil's familiars were holding court, but she would not be dissuaded.

She told him her cat, whom she named Joan, was a warrior of cats and caught mountains of rats and mice.

The corners of his mouth pulled up, and then he found himself laughing. The child jumped at the noise; 'twas rare Richard laughed. Mostly, he liked to stomp about and bellow.

In the end, Joan became the castle mouser, and Richard told Garrick that the child would make a great general in the king's army one day.

But then there were more cats—kittens, since Joan was with child. The blasted cat had five kittens. He found one of the men carrying one of the wee beasties with him as he walked the battlements.

The horse snorted, pawing the ground, as a man ran toward Richard, chased by three men.

The men stopped upon seeing him, crossed themselves, and, he imagined, swore heartily at the loss of their prey.

As the man drew nigh, Richard urged the horse forward. 'Twas not a man but a woman dressed in strange hose. The woman called out but was too far away for him to make out the words. Almost to her, he saw her fall.

He reined the horse in and leaned over. "Take my hand, woman." He reached out as she got to her feet. "Mistress. Come quickly—there may be more men."

She took his arm. Richard swung her up behind him and turned his horse to face the men.

"She is ours. We found her. Give her back," one of the men shouted.

Richard looked out from under the ever-present hood. "You dare to face the Beast of Bainford? Come then, let me drag you to hell." He wielded his sword, the muscles in his arm flexing as he ignored the gasp behind him. The men turned and fled.

From behind, Richard heard her teeth chattering. "You're...you're the beast?"

"Aye."

The woman tried to see around his back, but he held her firm. "Nay, mistress. I would not wish you to fall."

He could smell the fear rolling off her. "I ask for sanctuary." The words were soft in the still air.

She was a brave lass to ask for shelter, knowing his reputation.

"Where is your escort?"

"It's a really long story, and I'm really cold and tired."

The words sounded different when she spoke them, softer, sweet to his ears. She was no noble, nor was she from anywhere he knew. For the first time in a long while, Richard found himself curious. He would see her settled in the chair by the fire and find out what had brought the lass to his gates.

CHLOE COULDN'T BELIEVE her luck. This was the beast she'd heard so much about? On the horse, he looked like a knight straight out of a fairy tale. The only thing missing was the suit of shining armor.

He was strong enough to swing her up on the horse with one arm and wasn't even breathing heavily. She'd caught a glimpse of black fabric covering one eye, half of his face hidden by the hood of his cloak. The guy radiated warmth like an electric blanket turned to high, and she pressed against him, trying to get warm. If he would have said one rude thing, she would have said she was trying not to fall off the horse. The guy was solid as the stone walls in front of them.

It was a real, living, breathing castle. There was a tall wall with arrow slits for defense, and some of the construction looked new, as if large sections of the wall had fallen down and been repaired. They came to a drawbridge that also looked new, the horse's hooves clattering as the animal sped up, anxious to eat his dinner.

Her stomach rumbled. There was dark water, almost black, partially frozen, surrounding the castle. Chloe hoped the human waste didn't end up in there. If it did, everyone would probably get E.coli or something else disgusting. As she was sniffing to see if the water smelled like sewage, a fish jumped out in the middle where the water wasn't yet frozen, and she laughed at how silly she was acting. Obviously this was a moat used to stock fish for the castle, so it wouldn't have sewage in it. The garderobe waste would go into barrels that would be emptied somewhere else…if what her granda had told her held true.

"You find my home amusing?" he rumbled.

"I wasn't laughing at your home. It's fierce and forbidding. I was laughing at the little fish jumping. He looked as cold as I feel."

"The moat supplies us with plenty of fish to eat. He is used to the water. But you, mistress, are shivering enough to make me cold. Soon you will be warm."

Then the man chuckled, a rusty-sounding noise, like he didn't laugh much. "I will feed you. I hear how hungry you are—'tis a wonder I can hear over the noise."

Had the scary beast just made a joke? "Very funny. But you're right. I'm starved. I missed breakfast and lunch." No, Chloe corrected herself—she hated when other people got all judgey, so she'd wait and see before she called him a beast. Right now, he was a lot less scary than the rest of the men she'd encountered so far.

When they rode under the portcullis and were moving through the long stone tunnel, she heard the change in his breathing, could feel the tension in his body where she had wrapped her arms around him to keep from falling off the horse.

"Are you okay?"

"I do not care for small spaces," he said, stiffening in the saddle.

"This tunnel is a lot bigger than an elevator. I have a friend who is claustrophobic. Once she got stuck in a crowded elevator for three hours. She refuses to ride in an elevator to this day. Takes the stairs everywhere." Sara Beth had been almost catatonic when the fire department had finally rescued her. She didn't even like riding in small cars, but made an exception for the red MG if the top was down. "On the plus side, she has killer legs from all the stairs."

"What is 'okay'? What is an elevator?"

Oops. Chloe had to be more careful.

"Never mind," she mumbled, thinking about all the things and words she'd have to remove from her vocabulary. *You didn't think about when words came into usage until they were questioned. Try and talk like Granda does sometimes. Kinda old-fashioned and formal should do it.*

"What is your name, mistress?"

"I'm sorry. I was so busy being thankful you rescued me that I totally— I mean, I must have forgotten to tell you my name. I am Chloe Merriweather."

They rode through the grounds, her head on a swivel as she took in the blacksmith, a chapel, a long, low building, stables, and a few other rickety-looking structures. There were what she guessed were servants, going to and fro, and men fighting in an area she knew was called the lists. No one seemed particularly bothered by the snow or the cold.

"I am Richard. Lord Bainford."

So he was the beast. It was almost a bit disappointing. She'd been expecting something more along the lines of *Beauty and the Beast* than a cranky pirate knight.

CHAPTER 12

IF CHLOE HAD HAD any doubts she'd traveled through time, seeing the clothing the people wore, hearing the way they spoke, watching men fighting with real swords—all of those things together reinforced the truth. The stones had sent her through time. She was in an honest-to-goodness working castle. There wasn't any visible electricity. Not a single car, motorcycle, boat, airplane, or train. Not even a bicycle. Horses were the only mode of transportation, though she had spotted a few wagons and one carriage. The carriage did not look comfortable the way the big wheels jolted the carriage when they hit ruts in the road.

Chloe was so busy taking everything in, trying to commit every detail to memory so she could tell her granda, that she hadn't even noticed they'd stopped until the beast lifted her off the horse, like she weighed less than a bag of groceries, and set her firmly on the ground.

A young girl was waiting to greet them.

"Merry," he said. "Fetch blankets and spiced wine. The lady is going to break her teeth if we do not warm her."

"Aye, my lord." The girl scurried away to do his bidding.

"Come." He didn't wait to see if Chloe followed him as he strode into his home. Well, he certainly had the bossy lord thing down pat.

Chloe couldn't feel much of her body as she stumbled into his home and into a huge room.

The great hall was bustling with activity. What looked like old, weathered wood picnic tables were in the process of being pulled away from the walls and set up in long rows with benches on either side for seating. Her stomach grumbled again as the delicious smell of food filled her nose.

He led her to the kitchens. The warmth made her want to curl up in front of the roaring fire. Chloe groaned as the tingling spread from her toes and fingers through her body as she defrosted, dripping water onto the stone floor while steam rose from her clothes.

"Rest, mistress." The young girl Chloe had seen outside set a cup of wine in front of her, the wood tabletop worn smooth by countless hands over the years. The smell of spices hit her nose, making her mouth water.

"Merry, right?" Chloe took a sip, the warmth spreading through her veins. "Thank you."

Chloe looked to Richard, who was standing with his feet shoulder width apart, arms crossed over his chest, and the hood was still up. She could tell he'd suffered some kind of injury but couldn't get a close enough look to tell what kind.

"I cannot thank you enough for saving me from those awful men."

Finally warm, she pulled the heavy cloak off and hung it on a peg near the fire to dry.

There was a sharp intake of breath from Merry, but the girl quickly averted her eyes.

Richard, however, thoroughly looked Chloe up and down.

"We will have speech tonight. There is much to discuss, Mistress Chloe." She saw his lips move as he read her shirt. He blinked several times.

"'I'm not antisocial, I'd just rather read.' What is 'antisocial'?" Richard frowned at her shirt. "Why do you have words on your tunic?" He looked her up and down again, his eyes taking in every detail.

Chloe had the urge to smooth down her hair, but she resisted.

"Why are you dressed as a man? I have not seen such strange garments or shoes."

The wine went down fast, considering she didn't drink—wasn't old enough—but she'd been cold and it warmed her up, even though it tasted a bit like fruit and vinegar. Tart. Chloe held the cup up, grateful when Merry refilled it.

This man was too observant for his own good.

"Let me see. Antisocial means I like to be alone." She held up two fingers. "Where I come from, lots of people have words on their clothing. It is a way to express yourself." The third finger went up. "All women wear pants and shoes like mine. Your garments look odd to me." She smiled sweetly at him. "Any more questions?"

"Where is your escort, mistress?"

That was what she got for asking instead of keeping her big mouth shut. Luckily, Chloe was saved by her own stupidity. She'd put the cloak too close to the flames, and it had caught fire.

There was a commotion, everyone jumping into action to put out the fire before she burned down the kitchens. "I'm so sorry. I'm just exhausted. It's been a horrible twenty-four hours."

"You needs rest. I will see you to a chamber before you set fire to the rest of my home."

Chloe stuck her tongue out at his back, knowing it was childish, but happy when Merry and another little girl giggled. An adorable kitten ran past them as he led the way. Chloe wanted to pick up the cute little cat, but Richard was walking so fast that she practically had to jog to keep up. The guy was six two or six three to her five six, and he had long legs.

He still hadn't removed his hood, making her desperately curious to know what had happened. They wound around and around up the dim stairs to the second floor.

"Watch your step; many of the chambers have not yet been repaired." He sounded gruff and embarrassed.

They came to a stop at the end of the long hallway that was lit with actual torches. Though the walls were bare stone, they hadn't been painted, and there weren't any paneling or tapestries on the walls, either. Was he one of those nobles with a title but no gold?

The heavy wooden door swung open with a creak.

"Your chamber." He stepped into the room and made quick work of building up the fire. Chloe wanted to tell him to slow down so she could figure out what he did, but he was already finished. She'd have to hope one of the servants would take care of it or show her what to do. Especially because she'd lost the small book of matches somewhere along the way.

"Thank you for your hospitality."

He nodded. "More snow will fall this night. You would have frozen outdoors."

He crossed the room but paused in the doorway. "Rest. I will send someone to wake you before supper."

"Thank—" she called out, but he was already out the door. Guess he wasn't one for small talk. Neither was she. It wasn't a bad trait, except when she wanted lots of information.

The room was a bit small. The bed had linens and pillows, along with a wool covering, but they all looked shabby. Like they'd been in storage a long time and moths had gotten at them. But at least the room was clean. There was a pipe sticking out of the wall with running water. Chloe drank deeply, grateful for the water. There was a ewer and basin on a table, and a small trunk at the foot of the bed. Outside the window, she could see the woods, the landscape silver and white in the fading afternoon light.

Exhausted, she climbed into bed, only stopping to kick off her shoes. She was asleep before her head hit the down-filled pillows.

CHAPTER 13

"MISTRESS?"

Chloe woke to see a little girl holding a striped kitten. She yawned. "What a little cutie."

"His name is Moo because he meows at the cows. He believes he is a cow." The girl giggled. "I'm Maron. 'Tis time for supper. His lordship would have you join him in the hall."

Chloe smoothed her hair down, grateful there wasn't a mirror. After getting wet and sleeping on her hair, she must look like Medusa.

Maron frowned. "You wear hose?"

Time for the first of many lies to come. "For traveling. I lost my clothes, so I don't have a gown to wear to supper."

The girl had to be six or seven but acted much older. "My lord will see you have proper clothes befitting a lady."

Chloe followed Maron, listening to a constant stream of chatter revolving around her bratty brother, the kitten, and how much she liked living at Bainford, even though she missed her mama.

What she omitted was just as fascinating to Chloe. Not a word was uttered about Richard being the beast, or about his face. The few of his people she'd met thus far were loyal, and that said a lot about the man.

At one end of the hall, there was a raised dais with a table and tablecloth. In the middle of the table she saw Richard with his hood still in place. Was it on account of her, or did he always keep it up?

When she was close, he guided her to the seat on his left and pulled the chair out for her.

"Did you sleep well?"

"Yes. I feel much better."

Servants brought in bread—no pebbles included, thank goodness—and delicious, tangy cheeses. There must have been around thirty or forty people, counting the guards and all the kids.

He poured her a cup of wine.

"The wine is excellent," she said.

"The cellar is well stocked."

She noticed the holes in the tablecloth and wondered if he was one of those guys obsessed with wine. It would explain the state of his hall. Most of the people eating at the lower tables had their own knives. Chloe hoped Richard would either have an extra knife or let her borrow his. When the servants brought out the food, she exhaled. It looked like chicken pot pie, and there were spoons.

Her stomach let out a roar. Embarrassed, Chloe felt warm all over as she saw the corner of Richard's mouth turn up, as if pulled by a string. He pushed the dark hood back and stared at her. Daring her to flinch or scream or something.

Instead, Chloe forced herself to take a drink of wine, to not react. The damage was horrible. There was scarring around the black fabric he wore to cover his eye, which she now knew he must have lost. Half of his eyebrow was missing and there was terrible scarring down the side of his face. She'd seen similar damage in a classmate who'd been in a car that caught fire. It looked like it had happened a few years ago —the scars were faded, not an angry red or pink like on her classmate.

He had been devastatingly good-looking before. The candlelight turned his hair colors of fall. Chestnut, mahogany, and copper. The eye she could see was a dark blue, full of intelligence, and matched the blue of his tunic and hose.

She smiled at him and took a bit of the chicken pot pie. He kept refilling her glass. She wasn't used to so much wine and knew she was getting tipsy when she wanted to stand up and tell everyone all about planes, trains, and cars, and that they had a queen for a monarch, not a king.

"You have food in your belly and are dry and rested," Richard said. "Let us have speech. Where is your escort, Mistress Chloe?"

Richard startled her, and the wine sloshed over the cup, staining the tablecloth red.

He patted his mouth with an edge of the tablecloth she hadn't spilled on. "Tell me your tale." He leaned back in the chair, stretching out, looking every inch the fallen pirate king.

She'd been thinking about her story. Keeping it real enough, she wouldn't get confused, but not so real that he would think she was a faerie or witch.

"I have relatives near Lancashire. That's where I was going when I was assaulted at a tavern where we'd stopped for the night. My escort and I were separated, along with my belongings."

"Lancashire, you say. Where were you coming from?"

She could almost see him filing away every detail. Why had she had so much to drink?

"The Cotswolds." She wiped her mouth with the tablecloth as others were doing, avoiding the spill.

"'Tis a rather large area."

"Tetbury," she said, remembering one of the market towns that thrived in the wool trade during medieval times.

He looked unconvinced but let it go. She'd said Lancashire instead of Blackpool, figuring it might be more familiar, as Blackpool was a small coastal hamlet.

He poured more wine. "What are the names of your relatives?"

"I'm going to Falconburg Castle to see my great-aunt, Melinda Merriweather. Do you know her?"

"I have heard of Falconburg but do not know its lord. What is her husband's name?"

"Lord Falconburg." *Nutella on toast.* Chloe knew the story of how they'd found out the king had been at Falconburg for a Christmas dinner. What was Melinda's husband's name? There had been a guest list. She knew this. Darn it. Too much wine had made her fuzzy.

Careful to keep his good side to her, he frowned. "His given name."

"James Rivers." Ha. That was it.

"The Red Knight. I know him by reputation." Richard shifted in the chair. "I will send a missive."

"Thank you. I am sure they will be wondering where I am. Might you have men who could take me? I can pay them." She looked around the hall while she waited for him to answer. Four hearths were set into the walls, large enough for twenty people to stand next to each other, and the fires crackled merrily. High above, there were windows to let in light. Not much at this time of year, but at least it wasn't totally gloomy. There weren't any tapestries on the walls or rugs on the floor, and, quite frankly, the whole place smelled like it needed a good cleaning. The overall effect was shabby and unkempt.

The kids and servants blatantly stared at her, while his guardsmen were more discreet. Proper clothes would help her blend in, let her move around and observe. She reached for her phone for the hundredth time.

"Is there a cloth merchant? The loss of my clothing… I would like a gown. My jeans—hose were only to travel, not meant for all to see."

He drummed his fingers on the table. "You are my guest." He looked at her t-shirt. "The merchant will be here on the morrow. I will have gowns fashioned for you."

"Thank you." Chloe beamed at him, feeling happy and light, almost like she was floating above her body. This was going to be easier than she thought. It was too bad she couldn't stay a while longer. She thought of the phrase "still waters run deep" when she looked at him. She wanted to get to know him better. He couldn't be much older than her, but he had an old soul. It seemed like he carried the weight of the world on his shoulders.

No. She shook her head. Mustn't lose sight of why she was here. She had to get to Falconburg and meet Melinda. Then she would go home and fondly remember her adventures in the past, preferably after a long, hot shower, a pizza, and at least half a day catching up on texts and social media.

After supper, Richard offered her his arm. "Allow me to escort you to your chamber."

"Dinner was really good." She yawned, tired and restless at the same time. Was this what being tipsy felt like?

He was quiet on the way to her room. Being a bit shy and quiet, Chloe liked that the silence didn't feel forced. It was comfortable.

Did he know he hadn't put his hood back up? Or had he figured she now knew what he looked like, so why bother? She wanted to tell him not to be self-conscious, that we all carried scars, some on the outside, others deep on the inside.

But she didn't know him well enough to offer an opinion without being asked. Grammy Mildred had taught her just because you had an opinion, it didn't mean you needed to share it with the world. She thought people not minding their own business was a big part of what was wrong with the world. Chloe wished Gram and Granda could meet Richard.

At the door, she took a deep breath. She had to know without a doubt. To hear it said out loud so she'd be sure she wasn't going batty.

"Um…what year is it?"

"You do not know the year, yet you know from whence you came and where you are going?"

"I'm really tired. I did tell you what happened to me."

"Why were you pursued by ruffians?" he said, not quite believing her but too polite to call her a liar. At least, that was her guess as to what was going on behind that poker face of his.

"It doesn't matter, I'm safe now." Seeing his expression, she added, "If you really must know, I'll tell you tomorrow after breakfast." She touched his arm. "I bumped my head. Some things are clear, others not so much."

Either her answer satisfied him or he was enough of a gentleman not to call her on it.

"'Tis the Year of Our Lord 1337."

Chloe was glad she still had her hand on his arm, or she might have fainted at the confirmation of what she'd figured out. Now she had to find Melinda, because Chloe didn't know where the other Merriweather women lived and her granda had already gone to the future. If only she could figure out how the stones worked so she'd know how to get home after she'd met her relative. Her head was woozy, the doorway to her room tilted. Too tired to think about it, she smiled at Richard.

"Good night, Lord Bainford."

"Richard." He cleared his throat. "Sleep well, Mistress Chloe."

"Just Chloe," she said.

"Chloe."

She stood against the bolted door for a long time before climbing into bed.

CHAPTER 14

THE DREAM WAS SO realistic that Chloe woke panting. Though in her dream, the man who'd grabbed her in the tavern had dragged her out into the snow and raised a dagger. Then she woke, twisted in the sheets, panic filling her until she remembered. She was safe. Richard had rescued her.

Almost like the fairy tales where she always had a starring role, her very own knight had ridden out and plucked her from danger. Mind you, he wasn't wearing armor, and he was grouchy—oh right, and they didn't fall in love at first sight.

A small giggle escaped as she thought of one of her all-time favorite movies, *Enchanted*. She too had fallen into another world and found her other half. Chloe blamed her granda for ruining her for all the high school guys.

Oh…that was smart. Maybe he'd done it on purpose. She rolled her eyes. It would be like him to keep her a kid as long as he could. They had a lot to discuss when she made it back home.

The castle was quiet, everyone asleep, the fire burning well enough that she knew a servant must have come in and checked on it sometime while she'd been asleep. Her nose was cold, while the rest of her was toasty warm under the covers. The thought of touching the stone floor with her bare feet made Chloe put it off as long as possible, but eventually she knew that she'd have to find the bathroom...make that the garderobe.

With a small yelp, she ran across the icy floor and down the hall— wearing her t-shirt and jeans, since no one had loaned her anything to sleep in. Guess she had to wait until the merchant showed up in the morning. Robin had pointed out the facilities when he'd followed his sister, Merry, earlier.

Finished seeing to her needs and extremely happy she'd found a fabric padded seat instead of cold stone, Chloe ran back to her chamber, but paused by the basin and ewer.

She'd been so tired that for the first time since she could remember, Chloe had gone to bed without brushing her teeth. Her teeth felt scummy and rough when she ran her tongue over them. There was enough light from the fire to see, and if she didn't brush them, she'd think about it the rest of the night. Wrinkling her nose, she eyed the twig. The paste reminded her of that baking soda toothpaste her gram liked.

It was gritty but got the job done, and her teeth felt clean and smooth.

Back in bed, she pulled the bed curtains, shutting out the light. They made a huge difference in keeping her warm.

The next morning, Chloe thought if she could change one thing in the past, it would be hot showers. Water heated in a small pot over the fire and the tiny lump of weird-smelling soap worked, but it wasn't even close to hot water and gardenia-scented body wash.

Grateful there wasn't a mirror to show her how wild her hair must look, Chloe put on the same clothes she'd worn since arriving. She'd been studying the dresses and aprons the women and girls wore, thinking about what she'd wear to fit in while she was in the past.

Apparently, she'd slept in. The hall was almost empty, most of the tables and benches already pushed back against the walls. With a grumble, her stomach let her know what it thought about missing breakfast. She'd kill for a Pop-Tart.

"Mistress, come break your fast."

"Good morning, Robin."

The boy looked to be around twelve years old. He had a bit of dirt smudged on his chin and a rip in his hose.

"Looks like you've already been up for a while," she said.

He looked over his shoulder, grinning. "Aye. 'Twas my turn to empty the waste barrels, but I wrestled Tom and Jim." He jumped in the air. "I won. They have to empty the barrels for a se'nnight."

"Good for you." She smiled, seeing him jump and hop all the way to the kitchens.

"It smells so good in here." Chloe took a seat nearest the fire, on a stool at the table.

A bowl of what looked sort of like oatmeal was placed before her. As she watched, Merry drizzled a bit of honey on top.

"Thank you."

"Aye." She popped her brother on the arm with the wooden spoon. "I had to hide your porridge so this one wouldn't eat it all."

Robin pretended to pout. "Can I go now? Richard is breaking the new stallion this morn."

"Off with ye," his sister said. She bustled around the kitchens, looking like she'd been cooking all her life.

The porridge was tasty and filling. Chloe sipped the water Merry gave her, grateful the girl remembered. It was too early to drink ale, even if it was watered down. The thought of wine made her throat close up. Her head still pounded.

"How old are you, Merry?"

"I have twelve years, mistress." Merry wore a kerchief on her hair, and her apron was already dotted with flour as the girl formed loaves of bread.

"Twelve? I thought you were older. You're in charge of the kitchens?"

The girl continued to work, a few other little girls coming in and out while they talked.

"Aye. My da came to best the beast. He wagered us."

Chloe gasped, but the girl went on as if she hadn't heard.

"Robin and I were afeared of the beast, but then we saw him. He had kind eyes." She stopped to shoo a cat away from the hearth then turned back to Chloe. "Our da beat us. My lord does not beat us." She wrinkled her nose, pursing her lips. "He is fearsome when he bellows and when he fights. His face is ugly, but he is good to us. My brother and I will serve him well."

Loyalty. Chloe respected that. She knew beatings were common in medieval times, that children and women were treated differently, but to hear it spoken so matter-of-factly made her appreciate her own time even more.

She scraped the last bit of porridge from the wooden bowl. "That was delicious. I'll wash the bowl if you'll show me where."

"Nay, mistress." Merry shook her head. "Jane will see it done."

Knowing when she'd been dismissed, Chloe got up with a smile. The kid was twelve and already ran the kitchen like a boss.

CHAPTER 15

RICHARD USED the hem of his tunic to wipe his brow, grateful for the cold air. The paltry swordplay of his new guardsmen left much to be desired as he worked his way through the lists until he was sweaty and his leg trembled.

"Again," he called out to the men as he sat on the stone bench and leaned against the wall. One of the men went down, rolled across the lists, behind a wagon, and shrieked like a lass.

"Womanly weeping will not save you, lad. If this 'twas a real battle, you would have lost your head. Again," Richard called out. The noise came again. 'Twas not a lad—'twas a lass. In mere moments, he was around the wagon to find his man standing over Mistress Chloe who was taking deep, gasping breaths.

"Damnation, man." His fist met the man's face. "You could have killed her."

"I am truly sorry, my lord." The man bowed his head, wiping the blood away. "Forgive me, lady."

Richard offered her a hand, her skin soft as silk in his palm. Dust covered her from head to toe as he hauled her to her feet. She held up a finger and bent over, hands on her knees, breathing heavily. 'Twas a moment before she could speak.

"I wasn't looking where I was going. My fault." She waved the man away.

He squeaked and fled when Richard glared at him. While she panted, he studied her. The ribbon she'd used to tie back her hair had come undone, the curls blowing in the wind.

"Your ribbon." He bent to fetch it before it blew away.

"I don't want to lose it or my hair will look like the chickens have been nesting in it at night."

The thought of a chicken sitting on her head made him smile. She tied her hair back as he watched, itching to wrap the curls around his fingers. Each one stuck out from her head in a different direction. He knew enough of women to know if he laughed, she would be most vexed.

Deep brown eyes met his, forcing Richard to stand his ground. He had removed his cloak to fight, leaving his visage exposed. To her credit, she did not scream nor run away.

He picked up his cloak from the bench and fastened it about her. "To keep you warm. 'Tis cold and you should not be out."

Her nose and cheeks were pink as she pulled the cloak against her.

"Shall I show you Bainford?" He proffered his arm. After he had saved his sire, one of the courtiers had taken pity on him and given him lessons on how to be chivalrous—not that it did him any good, but 'twas a way to pass the time and not think about the pain.

"I'd like that." She took his arm, her hand small and delicate.

"The lads repaired the garrison, the chapel, and the stables. They are most happy to work indoors and repair the towers." He pointed to the Irishmen, a few singing while they went about their labors, going in and out of his home.

In the stables, she fed the horses a bit of carrot, smiled over the chickens, and stopped to pet every dog and cat they passed.

"Come up to the battlements. From there, you can see everything."

He took hold of her hand as they climbed the stairs so she would not fall, her odd footwear making squeaking noises on the stone. Out on the roof, the wind blew, and he pulled the hood of his cloak up over her head to keep her warm. When he tucked a curl behind her ear, he noticed there was a tiny hole in each ear. He opened his mouth to ask, but she smiled at him, making him forget what he was going to say.

"It's beautiful up here." She turned around in a circle. "Which way is London?"

He turned her around and pointed. "To the east." She smelled of dust and cold, and he'd never thought a woman smelled lovelier.

"And Falconburg?"

"To the north and west." He turned her again.

"I thought I was good with directions, but since I've...been here, the truth is out." She grinned. "I'm awful at directions."

The weak sunlight hit her face, the tiny freckles across her nose he'd not noticed until now. Her skin was smooth, the color of honey, as if she had been outside every day letting the sun kiss her skin. The unmarked skin filled him with envy. And while she wasn't what most men would call beautiful, he found her most comely—too lovely to ever want someone as ugly as he.

"How old are you?" She tilted her head up.

"A score and three."

"You seem older. I guess because you're responsible for all this." She gestured to the courtyard and lands below.

"And you? How many years have you, Chloe?"

"I'm eighteen."

"So old? Why are you not married with a household and babes of your own? Did you flee your husband? Are you a widow?"

She narrowed her eyes and scowled at him. "Did you just call me an old maid?" She poked him in the chest. "Listen to me. Where I come from, women choose when they want to get married, if ever. And no one tells them who they have to marry or if they have to have kids." She paced the battlements, her cheeks a fetching shade of pink.

"Flee my husband," she mumbled. "I do not have a husband, and no, I'm not a widow." She sounded rather remarkably as he did when he was vexed. "You know, I know things are different now, but the way you asked me, it wasn't very nice."

A curl escaped and was blowing in the wind. Richard reached out and tucked it behind her ear. "I did not mean to offend. I am unused to company."

"Sorry. I didn't mean to get all huffy. It's just my friend, Sara Beth, her mom thinks if you don't have a husband by the time you finish college, you won't ever find one." She clapped a hand over her mouth.

"College?"

"I meant university."

Now 'twas his turn to gape at her. "You go to university? A woman?" Richard could see her thinking. What was Mistress Chloe hiding? And why was she telling such tales?

She waved a hand around. "Never mind. I think I'm still a bit woozy from bumping my head. I don't know what I'm saying."

Hrumph. He did not believe the little shrew for one moment. In time he would find out what she was hiding, and if she meant him or those under his protection at Bainford harm.

"You said you were traveling to Lancashire to visit relatives when you and your escort were assaulted and separated. Along with your belongings?"

"Yes. That is what I said." Mistress Chloe suddenly found something in the sky that warranted her attention.

"And Lord and Lady Falconburg are expecting you?"

She fidgeted. "That's correct."

"The Red Knight would take my head if I do not see you well cared for. You will tell me about the ruffians."

"I'll be sure to tell them how kind you've been." She looked into the courtyard. "Look, it's Moo."

"Moo? I see no cattle." Had the lass gone daft?

"No, Moo is a kitten." She touched his arm, then pointed.

He followed her direction to see the wee beast.

"Look. He's stalking the chicken."

The wee cat was indeed. Then the hen turned and scared the animal, who ran for the safety of the stables.

Mistress Chloe's laugh filled the air.

"The ruffians, mistress?"

She sighed. "Somehow, a man— I think he was a noble by the way he was dressed. You should have seen his sleeves—they were this wide." She opened her arms.

"Aye. I have seen such garments. 'Tis not practical to fight wearing such a tunic."

"No kidding. It's how I got away. He had climbed into my bed—"

"What?" he roared. "This man defiled you?"

"Oh my gosh, lower your voice." She hunched down as a few of the men looked up at them. "No. He did not. Though I think he planned to." She touched the stone walls, not meeting his gaze. "That's how I got away. I yanked on his sleeves, and when he fell off the bed, I kicked him and ran." She looked at the ground. "I think it was my fault. I went to use the...garderobe in the night and must have forgotten to bolt the door. That's how he got into my room. Then I was chased again in the woods. I got lost, was chased again, and during that time, I hit my head, so some things are hard to remember."

"Such as losing your escort and forgetting what year it is?"

"Exactly." She smiled at him. "It's getting awfully cold up here. We should go inside. Do you think it will snow today?"

"Come. I will see you settled in front of the fire with a cup of wine." He knew she did not wish to talk of what had happened to her. The woman had been running with men chasing her. She was scared, but she was not telling him everything.

Richard had grown up with other children like him and learned to survive by his wits and his fists. Mistress Chloe was up to no good, and he was going to discover why she was really at Bainford. If she meant to betray him, he would cast her out of the gates and leave her for the wolves to eat.

CHAPTER 16

WHEW, that had been close. Chloe held on to Richard's arm as he led her from the battlements down the stairs and into his solar.

"I have built up the fire and sent for wine, my lord." Richard's steward, Edwin, looked older than her granda with his white hair and brown eyes, but she couldn't be sure. The few women who worked at the castle were all younger than they looked. Either the product of a hard life or not enough moisturizer.

Growing up at the beach, Chloe was a big believer in sunscreen and moisturizer. What would happen if she didn't make it home in time to start school? Would the college hold her place or give it to someone else? No, she couldn't think about home right now. If she did, she'd cry, and Richard could not stand womanly weeping.

One of the boys brought them wine, along with a bit of cheese and bread. When the child put the tray down, he stopped chewing, an innocent look on his face. It took everything Chloe had not to bust out laughing.

She passed a goblet of wine to Richard. "I don't think my feet have been warm since I arrived." She kicked off her sneakers and wiggled her toes in front of the fire. There was a gurgling, and she looked at the boy in alarm, worried he was choking. Instead, she saw his little cheeks full of bread and cheese. He chewed a moment, then opened his mouth, the words coming out muffled around the food he hadn't yet swallowed.

"Mistress. Your toes. They are blue with cold." He bent down and took her foot between his hands, rubbing her feet so vigorously that she almost fell off the stool.

"My feet are cold but it's not that bad. My toes are painted."

The boy stopped and gingerly touched her big toe. "How do ye get the paint on your feet? Why would you paint your toes?"

A shadow fell over her legs as Richard leaned down to get a better look as well. "Aye. Tell us, Chloe."

Like she needed another thing to explain. As payback for drawing the attention of Mr. See All and Know All, she ratted out the kid. "Finish swallowing all the cheese and bread in your mouth, and I'll tell you."

"What have I told you about eating from the trays?" Richard scowled at the boy, who chewed furiously. Tomas gave her a look that promised retribution at a later time. She'd be sure to check her bed for a fish or dead mouse or whatever little boys did in this time period.

The kid swallowed and hung his head. "I'm sorry, my lord. I was hungry."

"Do it again and you'll be emptying the waste barrels for a fortnight. And cleaning up after the dogs and cats for another fortnight."

"I willna do it again, my lord."

Richard rolled his eyes. "Off with you."

"You have odd customs in Tetbury," he said to Chloe. "'Tis passing strange, for I have been there and did not see a soul dressed in such odd garments, or heard anyone talk with your accent."

Nosy busybody of a man. She smiled sweetly at him, using her best "I'm not doing anything" look she gave to teachers when she was texting Sara Beth instead of paying attention in class. "I wasn't born in Tetbury. I only lived there a short time."

"Where were you born?"

This was a bit trickier. She sent up a sorry to the universe for what she was about to say. "I'm from a land far, far away, across the ocean. It's called America. We were sailing to England when there was a terrible storm and the ship went down. My parents died and I was left in the care of a distant relative."

"More distant relatives." He looked at her for so long that Chloe squirmed under his gaze. "I am sorry for your loss. My dam died when I was but six."

Now she felt awful, but she couldn't very well have him sending out messengers to try and tell her nonexistent family she was safe.

"I'm sorry. Is your father living?"

His face darkened. "Nay." Then he abruptly got up and strode to the door. "I shall fetch you for dinner." With that, the door banged shut behind him, leaving her alone with her thoughts.

After dinner, she was sitting on the floor of the hall with several of the kids, playing with half a dozen kittens, when the merchants arrived. Two of Richard's guardsmen led them in, and the man himself had his cloak on and the hood up—something he did when he went out or strangers came to the castle.

The merchant was short and round, with dirty blond hair. He'd brought a young girl with him, and the girl had the same nose and eyes. She had to be his daughter. He looked around the hall as if committing every detail to memory to tell everyone at the pub afterward. Chloe narrowed her eyes, the merchant already losing points with her.

"Shall we begin? I have lovely silks for gowns, lace, and ribbon."

Edwin stepped forward. "You may display your wares here." He motioned to where several tables had been left out after dinner. There were clean tablecloths on them to protect the man's wares.

The man clapped his hands together at the children helping. "Careful—do not let the cloth touch these filthy floors."

Oh no, she didn't like him at all. She'd gone with her mom once to see the local laundromat owner at her home. Her mom created amazing websites and often would meet clients at their business or home. The lady was a serious hoarder, and the house smelled, but Chloe knew not to say a word about the state of the woman's home.

She and her mom simply pretended the towering piles weren't about to fall on their heads.

Richard didn't bellow at the man; he kept to the shadows around the perimeter of the hall, skulking around like he was embarrassed to be seen.

There was a young boy as well. Chloe had missed him behind the bolts of fabric. With the matching nose and eyes, he had to be the son.

The kids quickly laid out the fabrics, the silks shimmering in the firelight. She walked up and down the tables, looking at the offerings.

"The silk is beautiful, but I won't be going to court, so I really need practical, everyday gowns." She had her money split between her pockets. Even though Richard said he'd pay for her dresses, she didn't want him to use his gold, since she was planning on leaving.

The man was five or six inches shorter than she and still managed to look down his nose at her. His clothing was a muted blue and beautifully tailored, so she was hopeful he was good at his job.

"As the lady wishes." He made it sound like an insult. Out of the corner of her eye, she noticed Richard had taken a couple of steps closer.

She looked at the ribbon and picked out several colors to tie her hair back and keep it from sticking out in a million directions. Most of the girls and women at the castle wore muted browns and grays, with a few blues. The natural color apron over the dresses made a nice combination. They still had the upper two floors to clean, and she wanted to travel without attracting too much attention, so she needed simple gowns.

As to what else she needed, Chloe was a bit lost. There was a gasp and a shriek. The man's eyes were huge, and his daughter hid behind his legs.

"Is there a mouse?" Chloe stared at him, hands on her hips.

"Nay…l…l…lady," the man stuttered. He kept darting glances from her to Richard, who had appeared next to her without a sound.

Without looking at the man, Richard snarled, "She lost her belongings and will require a cloak, two shifts, gowns, and silk hose."

"Of course, Lord Beast." The man turned red. "Lord Bainford."

Chloe had learned enough during her short time here that she thought the man should be jumping up and down at such a sale instead of looking at Richard like he was on display in a zoo.

If she didn't need clothes so badly, she would have thrown him out herself. The wool was nice and heavy and would keep her warm. She looked at the offering of colors, surprised at the amount of choice. Everything from the muted colors to bright blues, reds, and purples.

"Richard?"

He was at her side in an instant. She must have looked overwhelmed, because he took charge, issuing orders, sending everyone scurrying about. Before she knew it, she'd been measured, and the material for her aprons, hose, and shifts had been selected and placed next to the ribbons for her hair. He had picked out a dark brown for her cloak and ordered it trimmed with fur. He said the girls at Bainford would embroider it for her.

Grateful for the help, she picked out a dark, almost burgundy red and a heather gray. "I think these will do nicely."

The man nodded.

"One more thing." She explained how she wanted pockets in the apron and the gowns. He was confused until she picked up a corner of the fabric and demonstrated.

"Ah, yes. It will be done."

Chloe touched Richard's sleeve, and when he bent down, she whispered in his ear. His eyebrow went up, but he nodded.

"See a tunic and hose fashioned in the same colors for the lady."

The man gaped. "'Tis not proper. She—"

"Do as I say." He thundered.

The man gulped and nodded. "Yes, my lord."

She tried to pay, but Richard wouldn't let her. "Nay, the Red Knight will be indebted to me for taking care of you."

"Thank you." As much as she was dying to know more about Melinda's husband, she couldn't ask without giving herself away, and he was already suspicious.

By the way Richard acted, Chloe knew he must be used to people treating him like he wasn't a man but an oddity about which they could say whatever they wished, with no thought to hurting his feelings.

His jaw was clenched so tight that she thought it a wonder he hadn't cracked his teeth. It was the only indication he was affected by the man's behavior.

She wondered what the merchant would have done if he'd seen Richard without his hood. Though the little pumpkin of a man kept trying to get a better look. At one point, she tripped him and pretended it was an accident. Not nice, but she didn't want anyone treating Richard as lesser.

CHAPTER 17

THE RIBBONS CHLOE could take now; the rest would be delivered in a few days. She was admiring the colors as she placed them in the trunk when there was a knock at the door.

Richard stood in the doorway, a bundle in his arms. "I had one of my tunics and hose cut down to fit you until your gowns are ready." He looked at her clothes. "Your garments attract undue attention, even for Bainford. I would burn them if 'twas me, but if you must keep them, put them in the trunk and lock it." Then he handed her a pair of beautiful leather boots and a pair of knitted socks. "For you."

The black tunic and hose were soft from being laundered, the leather soft and supple. The socks were a natural color. Her toes would finally be warm.

"This is too much, thank you. I'm sorry if I've caused you any trouble."

"Nay. You bring light to Bainford." He filled up the room with his presence. She noted the daggers in his boots, the sword at his hip, and thought of her granda, who always had a dagger somewhere on his person.

"When you have dressed, I will walk with you on the battlements," he said. "I know you like to look at the snow and the land."

"That would be lovely. I won't be long."

He shut the door behind him, and she held the clothes to her nose. They smelled like him. The scent of the woods, leather, and the outdoors. If she could bottle it, she'd make a fortune.

The tunic was long enough to be a dress, and the hose sagged a bit around the knees, but otherwise, the girls had done a great job. Then Chloe noticed a small detail and laughed. One of them had embroidered a cat chasing a ball of string on the sleeve. The socks were warm and the boots fit well. All she needed was a dagger and she'd feel very medieval.

Her sneaker mules were trashed, but she didn't dare burn them—the smell would be horrible—so she put them on the stool and folded her clothes on top of them. She'd ask for the clothes to be laundered and then she'd pack them in the trunk in the knapsack she'd found in there. The sneakers couldn't be buried—what if she needed them to get home? To be safe, she'd wash them herself; no sense in having the girls look too closely at the laces or the tag inside. Maybe she'd better wash the jeans and t-shirt too; the zipper on her jeans would cause way too many questions.

A blue ribbon that reminded her of Richard's eyes went around her hair, tied in a low ponytail. Comfortable, she opened the door only to find him there, one booted foot touching the wall, arms crossed as he leaned against the wall.

"I didn't know you were waiting right here. I would have hurried." Was it hot in here? Or was it him?

"I would gladly wait all day." He proffered his arm. "Shall we?"

RICHARD HAD BESTED the three men who had ridden through his gates and demanded to fight the beast without breaking a sweat. The gold would pay for him to replant the gardens and the orchards in the spring.

Restless, he had run through the rest of his guard and spent the day teaching the lads swordplay.

He removed his sweat-soaked tunic and wiped his face when Chloe entered the solar bearing a cup of ale. Richard liked her watching him as he fought. Knowing she was there, he'd fought harder, caring what she thought, and did not want her to look upon him with revulsion.

"I'll fetch you more ale." She turned and fled. Was his form as disgusting as his visage? A sigh escaped as he sat in the chair and brooded, his booted feet in front of the fire.

⚜

TWO WEEKS at Bainford Castle had Chloe totally revising her opinion. The serving girls she'd first encountered in the tavern were nothing more than gossips. They'd probably never even seen Richard, simply repeated and embellished the stories they'd heard.

Out of all the kids and servants, there were several adults who still crossed themselves whenever Richard passed by. The last time he'd fought for gold, she'd seen the looks, heard the whispers, and was so angry that she could hardly hand Richard the cup of ale without screaming. The man had been sitting in front of the fire, scars on his back and arms from the battles he'd fought in—the battles he'd fought to make money to keep everyone he was responsible for fed. And those jerks still couldn't see past his face.

Then today, she'd had enough. After the morning meal, she'd organized a cleaning crew to tackle the second floor. When they thought she was out of earshot, she'd heard them talking about Richard. To his face, they called him "my lord," but behind his back, they still called him the beast. They told tales of how the cats running around were the devil's familiars.

She should have laughed it off, but she was furious on his behalf. So she stomped down the stairs, yelling for Edwin.

"Mistress Chloe, I fear you have been spending too much time with my lord. You are beginning to sound like him." The steward winked at her.

"Sorry."

Edwin had been favoring his shoulder, rubbing it. One of her gram's friends, Esmeralda, had done the same thing, and said it was arthritis.

"I don't mean to pry, but your shoulder?" She kept her voice low, not wanting to draw attention to him, as she knew he did not like to complain. "Do you eat fish?"

He blinked at her. "Nay. I find I do not care for the taste."

"If you put heat on your shoulder at night it will help with the stiffness. So will willow bark tea." She smiled. "And fish."

"Think you?"

"A friend of my grandmother suffered from stiffness and aches. She said those three things helped a great deal. I know you do not care for fish. Let me talk to Merry and have her prepare it another way."

Edwin eyed her dubiously but nodded. "It canna hurt. Thank ye." He grinned at her. "Why were you stomping about and bellowing?"

"I've heard a few of the servants talking about Richard. I do not care for the things they say."

Edwin sighed. "'Tis hard to find those who will stay. Most run away."

"How can they say such mean things? I've seen the children left at the gates."

"Changelings." He nodded.

She scoffed. "Come on, you don't really believe that, do you?" Chloe had worn Richard's old tunic and hose instead of one of her gowns today, since she knew she'd be crawling around on the floors. It was so much easier to move around in pants than a long gown that caught on her heels and made her trip, much to the amusement of the kids.

"The parents believe the children are changelings. Now orphans come to Bainford in search of meals and a safe place to sleep. They are willing to face my lord." Edwin shrugged. "We need the servants. I am too old to care for Bainford alone."

"You don't believe the stories about him, do you?"

He chuckled. "Nay. I remember when he rode through the gates."

Edwin looked sad. "He was so angry, the wounds terrible, and yet for all his grumbling, he has done all in his power to be a good lord."

"I won't have the servants talking about him. Can you get rid of them?"

"Who will do the work?" Edwin rubbed his shoulder, wincing.

"Will you get rid of them?"

Edwin patted her arm. "I am an old man. They will not listen."

"The children are already doing most of the chores. The ones who are too young can take care of the cats and dogs. Chores will be good for them, keep them out of mischief."

Chloe was making it up as she went. Thanks to Gram, she hadn't had to do much growing up. The housekeeper cleaned and did the laundry, so that left making her bed every day and picking up her room so the housekeeper could clean.

Loading and unloading the dishwasher was also her responsibility. Her mom had offered to take over the cleaning, but Gram said no; her housekeeper had been with her for years and needed the work. So Chloe's mom ran errands, took care of the grocery shopping, and cooked.

Gram and Mom had wanted Chloe to enjoy being a kid. But now? She wanted to pay Richard back for the clothes and to let him know with actions that she noticed how he cared for others.

"The children and I can take care of Bainford." She pressed her lips together. "You won't stop me?"

"Nay, lady."

Full of purpose, Chloe gathered all of the servants and children together. She looked at each one, staring until they dropped their eyes.

"I have heard some of you talking about Lord Bainford. You have full bellies and a warm bed because of him, yet you gossip like the serving wenches in the village. I'll not have it." She went up to each person, one by one, that she'd heard talking about Richard. "All of you can leave. Do not return."

Two of the men scoffed. "Says you. We aren't going anywhere."

"You cannot make us leave." One of the women pouted.

Chloe stood there, hands on her hips, wondering how on earth she'd get them to leave if they refused. Then they straightened up.

"Mistress Chloe." Garrick and six guardsmen stood behind her, hands on their swords. "You heard her. Be gone."

The servants she'd dismissed grumbled and glared, but they left.

"See they leave, then close the gates," she ordered Garrick.

"I shall see it done." He waited until his men had followed the servants out before he leaned in close. "Does Richard know?"

She bit her lip. "No. What do I tell him? I don't want him to know it was because of the things I've heard them saying about him. It might hurt his feelings."

Garrick patted her shoulder, almost making her fall over. The man had no idea how strong he was. "Tell him they offended you. Who knows why women do what they do." He grinned.

Afterward, she told the remaining servants and children what their new duties would be, starting with readying the hall for supper.

Hands on her hips, Chloe surveyed a job well done. Contributing to the household made her feel like she wasn't taking advantage of Richard's hospitality. The great hall was pretty as a peach. Wait until Richard saw how the second floor would sparkle when they finished.

CHAPTER 18

"You, my friend, are getting fat and lazy, eating so well since Merry took over the kitchens," Garrick jested as he swung his sword, his hair plastered to his neck.

"I am not fat nor lazy, you insolent cur." Richard wielded his sword, muscles flexing as he lunged.

Garrick had come and gone over the past years, staying until he was required to fight. Knowing how much it pained Richard not to fight, his friend did not talk overmuch of the skirmishes.

They had been in the lists all morn. At times, the loss of his eye made Richard sick when he swung a sword. He would go a fortnight, mayhap two, when his leg and arm did not pain him, making him believe 'twas healed. But nay, 'twas merely the cursed fates jesting with him. For the next morn he would wake in a foul temper, his head and body aching.

Bent over and gasping for breath, he knew 'twas going to snow again. Ever since his injury, much like his steward, he knew when it would rain or snow by how much his leg and eye pained him.

When he stood, Richard blinked slowly until he no longer saw spots. Nay, no spots, but his servants leaving through the gates.

"What the bloody hell? Why do you leave Bainford and your lord?" he roared.

One of the men sneered. "The odd wench threw us out."

"Told us to leave and never show our faces at Bainford again, else she would see us run through," said another.

Chloe. Who did the wench think was to order his servants about as if they were her own? He was lord here, not her. Bainford was his home; he would not have a wench with odd ideas turn it upside down.

By his count, he was left with a few women and more than a score of young ones. Full of fury, Richard sheathed his sword.

"Where are you off to? You haven't paid me back for my insults." Garrick waited, sword at the ready.

Richard narrowed his eyes. "You knew?" The look on Garrick's face told the tale. "I will see to you later."

Richard's heavy steps into the hall had the lasses fleeing.

"Chloe. Come here," he thundered.

One of the little ones ran up the stairs with a squeak. While he waited, he paced back and forth across the hall until his anger was stoked higher than a bonfire.

She wiped her face with her apron, a damp tendril stuck to her cheek. "What's so important?"

"Are you chatelaine of Bainford?"

"Obviously not." She looked to the doors. "Oh, that's what you're yelling about." She turned her back on him. "I have work to do."

"Damnation, woman. You will face me when I speak to you."

She turned around, hands on her hips. "I don't care for your tone."

"I am lord of Bainford, not you. I have let you go around in my tunic and hose like a man, and have I said a word? Nay. And this is how you repay my hospitality? You turn out my servants without asking me."

She took two steps closer, brown eyes almost black, her entire face and neck pink as she poked him in the chest.

"Quit yelling at me and let me explain," she bellowed, sounding a bit like him. Tapping her foot, she blew a curl out of her eyes. "Don't be stupid. Of course I know you are lord here. For your information, those lazy servants don't do anything around here but laze about and gossip, and I won't have it."

"*You* won't have it?" He ran a hand through his hair. "You are not my lady wife. 'Tis not your place to turn out my servants."

"I wouldn't be your wife if you were the last man on the planet, you…you—"

"Go on, mistress. Say it."

"You ass!" She pushed him hard enough that he rocked back on his heels. 'Twas merely because she startled him. A woman was not so strong.

Richard leaned forward until he was close enough he could feel her breath on his face. "You were going to call me beast." He sneered at her.

"The hell I was, but you sure are acting like one. I was only trying to help. To get rid of those who love drama. They're toxic."

"Get out," he roared.

She took a step back, and the hurt on her face made Richard want to take back the words, knowing he was being an arse, but he was too angry.

Garrick and his guardsmen leaned against the walls of his hall, no doubt come to defend her. They followed her about like lads. His oldest friend placed a hand on his arm. "Richard, do not do this. Let me explain."

Richard shook him off. "Leave me be."

Two of the little girls were weeping. He could not bear the noise.

"Cease," he said, which only served to make them weep louder.

"Don't make them cry. You are so mean. To think I thought you were kind and nice." Chloe's eyes blazed.

"Why are you still darkening my hall? Get out or I will have you thrown into the moat." She gasped, as did several others. He scowled. "Get back to your labors, the lot of you."

Chloe ran up the stairs.

"You are an arse," Garrick said as he led the men outside, leaving Richard to ponder what he had done.

CHLOE PUSHED THE DOOR CLOSED, angry it was too heavy to slam. Why was he being so mean? They'd made so much progress. He'd been nicer to everyone lately.

She swiped at the tears running down her cheeks. Everyone had seen their fight. There was no way she could tell him she'd fired the servants because of what they said about him. She wouldn't hurt him like he'd hurt her.

Not even giving her the chance to explain, though? That he would think she was trying to take over? What did she know about running a castle? Not much. She was still figuring out how to clean.

Maybe he wasn't a beast in looks, but he sure was acting beastly. He'd made his feelings clear, and she wasn't staying where she wasn't wanted. Chloe pressed the heels of her palms into her eyes and breathed deeply. Once she had herself together and wasn't shaking, she went to the trunk and opened it, digging through everything until she came up with the knapsack. She pulled it out and added the gowns and the old tunic and hose, along with her extra shift and hose. Should she leave him some money to pay for the clothes?

With a shake of her head, she decided nope, the clothes would be payment for the work she'd done. Every coin was precious now that she would be traveling to Falconburg.

A small sob escaped as she looked at the hair ribbons. They too went in the bag. The coins were last. She split them between her boots, the pockets in her cloak, and the knapsack. That way, if she was robbed, hopefully they wouldn't get everything.

The beautiful cloak with the fur-trimmed hood and pretty embroidery made her heart hurt. She had begun to feel like she belonged. That if, for whatever reason, she couldn't get home, it would be okay.

Chloe squared her shoulders. Family was family. Once Melinda and her husband heard who Chloe was and about her predicament of being stuck in the past, they would take her in. She could be a nanny to their kids, or she could clean. Turned out she was pretty good at getting a dirty old castle to sparkle.

When she'd first arrived, the hall was a horrific mess. Chickens nested in the corners of rooms and the dogs and cats roamed freely— which was fine, but there was hair everywhere, and between them, the kids, and the men, there was a ton of mud and muck tracked in every day, which no one cleaned up. Now, though, the hall was clean, and kept clean every day.

With a last longing look at the fire in her chamber, she softly pulled the door closed behind her.

On her way out, Chloe went to the storage room. When they'd been cleaning, they'd found earthenware vessels one of the women told her they were pots to keep fire going while traveling. She took one, added twigs, and lit it from the fire in the kitchens.

Two of the little ones were asleep by the hearth. Careful not to wake them, Chloe took a metal cup she could use to melt snow for water. Bread and salted, dried fish also went into her pack. That would hold her until she found taverns that weren't scary. No way would she sleep in a tavern, not after the last time. She would eat and move on, finding someplace else to sleep. Where, she didn't know, but something would come to her.

No one stopped her. Chloe paused when she got to the portcullis, but no one said a word, and Richard didn't come for her to tell her he'd been an idiot.

It was cold, but at least it wasn't snowing, and the longer she was in the past, the less the cold bothered her. Chloe guessed she was getting used to it, though she missed the hot, humid days at the beach.

Walking to the north and west, she hoped, Chloe came upon an old shack. It was falling down, but at least it would provide her shelter for the night.

Not wanting to share the space with any critters, she stomped around, hoping it would be enough to scare them away. At least she didn't have to worry about snakes.

During her freshman year, a black snake got into school and terri- fied the girls for weeks, popping out of lockers and slithering under bathroom stalls before a boy caught it and took it outside. Chloe shuddered thinking about how she checked under the toilet seats each time she went, afraid it would be hiding there.

In place of a hearth was a ring of rocks. The wood outside was wet, so she picked up bits and pieces inside and used that for kindling. It was smoky inside, making her cough and gag, but soon enough she got used to it, only rubbing her eyes occasionally. At least she wouldn't freeze.

What was wrong with Richard? Did he really care she'd fired his help, or was it because he really didn't want her there and it was an easy excuse to get rid of her?

Gram's voice filled Chloe's head. *It wasn't your place to fire the help, even if it needed to be done. You overstepped and should apologize.*

Well, it wasn't like she was going to go back and beg. Forget it. Falconburg was her destination. The further away from Richard, the better.

CHAPTER 19

RICHARD WAS FULL. Supper filled his belly, the wine was plentiful, and his hall was clean, the rushes sweet.

"There are no chickens wandering about."

"You are an arse, Richard." Garrick scowled. "Why is your hall clean?" He rocked back in his chair. "Because Mistress Chloe made it so."

He was an arse. "One of the lads saw her going to the stables."

Garrick snorted. "I hope she filched one of your best horses."

"Don't be daft. You know she cannot ride well enough on her own."

Edwin passed by scowling at Richard. The bloody woman had bewitched everyone in his home. And he had been a fool.

Richard hunched his shoulders. "She will be warm in the stables. In the morn, I will bring her back." He saw the scorn on Garrick's face. "What? If I go now, she will try and slit my throat. The woman has a fearsome temper."

"Who does she remind you of?" Garrick said. "Damned whoreson."

Alone in his solar and deep in his cups, Richard comforted himself that he had done the right thing. He was lord of Bainford, had earned the title, the castle. Paid for it with the loss of an eye and the ever-present aches in his body. So why did he feel as if he was beneath contempt?

"Mistress Chloe will make some man a fine wife." Garrick drained his goblet of wine and poured them both another.

Hrumph. Richard would not think on her with another. The thought made him want to rend the lucky main in twain.

"She is hiding something. 'Tis good to know what she truly thinks of me." Richard didn't know if her secrets were those every woman kept or something else. He had not wanted to pry. *We all have our secrets.*

"Do you think she will go to Falconburg?" Garrick stared into his cup. "'Tis going to snow again. She'll be cold."

"Aye. She is always cold. Said she came from a village where 'tis always warm."

Richard had thought she would stay in her chamber and then he would fetch her for supper and tell her he was sorry for bellowing. That he had been in pain and taken it out on her. For the first time since he'd found her, she'd done what he had asked and left him. He missed the bothersome wench more than he knew, and she had not been gone a full day.

Garrick tapped his booted foot. "It would take her nigh on a month to travel to Falconburg if she is not killed or defiled or gets lost on the way. She is a woman traveling alone and not familiar with our lands."

Richard gritted his teeth. "Think you I don't know?" He frowned. "The men did not find her in the stables?"

Garrick shook his head, looking as miserable as Richard felt.

"Did the men search the chapel?"

"Aye. She was not there."

He shifted in the chair to ease the pain in his leg. She had taken her belongings and her odd clothes with her and would not return. Chloe was gone for good because he was a sorry bastard.

Garrick wiped his eyes, a look of agony upon his visage.

"What is it, man?" Richard said.

"You did not think to inquire as to why she turned out the servants."

"Nay. Why?" Richard gazed at Garrick. "Tell me."

"The servants she sent away…were those who… They called you beast, crossed themselves when you passed by, spread tales in the village."

Richard was stunned. "Why did she not tell me?"

Garrick snorted. "You were too busy bellowing at her to listen. She was angry they would talk of you so, said she would not allow them to spread such lies about a good man."

"She did this for me?" Damn the wench. He thought he was going to weep like a babe. 'Twas the nicest thing anyone had ever done for him. His fierce woman was protecting his damnable pride.

Richard slammed his hands on the table. "Take the men and the lads good at tracking rabbits. Find the wench."

"'Tis too late to go this night. The horses may break a leg in the dark. 'Twill have to wait until the morn," Garrick said softly.

This was a tragedy of immense proportions, and all of Richard's making. If something happened to her, he would never forgive himself.

"She is alone. The woman will freeze." He had been a dolt. When he found her, he'd drop to his knees and beg for a forgiveness he did not deserve nor expect her to grant. He would tell her she could dismiss any at Bainford if she would but come home.

᠃

FOR THREE DAYS THEY SEARCHED. The snow fell, growing deeper and deeper, making it nigh on impossible to track her. Where had the woman gone? 'Twas as if she had disappeared to go live with the faeries. Not that Richard believed in such things.

On the fourth day, they came upon the remains of an old hut. The blasted witless woman had gone the wrong way. She had traveled south for several miles instead of north and west.

"Mistress," Garrick called as they dismounted. Richard was stiff from riding, limping to the open doorway. It was small and dark inside, like the chapel when he was hurt.

Black spots appeared in front of him. *Nay.* Richard shook his head. To find Chloe, to bring her home safe, he would crawl through all the rubble again.

"Chloe," he said softly. "'Tis Richard. Are you there, lass?"

She appeared out of the darkness, her hair sticking out in all directions, brandishing a stick, a reproachful look on her lovely face.

When she saw 'twas him, she threw the stick to the side. Richard hauled her into his arms. Saints, he wanted to keep her always. She had terrified him worse than any battle.

"I was so scared. I heard noises. It's been days." Then she pulled away and pushed him, scowling. "I hate you."

"Aye. I am an arse. Let me in so I may beg forgiveness." He pulled her into the hut, breathing hard. 'Twas dim, but she had a fire going, and the holes in the roof and walls eased his discomfort enough that the spots and the feeling he would be ill did not return.

She saw him looking at the blaze. "I took a fire pot. It's been hard to keep it going—with no door and holes in the walls and roof, it hasn't helped much. I'm freezing. And something moved over there." Her eyes filled with tears. "Why did you send me away?"

"'Tis no excuse. I was in terrible pain and behaved like an arse. We have searched for you for three days. They have been the longest days of my life."

"I've been too scared to keep going." She was shivering.

He pulled her onto his lap in front of the paltry fire and held her close. "Nay, say no more. Let me warm you. This is one thing I can do without causing you pain."

Together they stayed close to the fire, not speaking. He did not have the words to tell her what she meant, what the thought of losing her had done to him.

He blew out a breath. "Have I told you how I lost my eye?"

She looked up at him, tears on her eyelashes. "Saving the king."

"Aye. I was fighting in Scotland." He touched the scars around his eye. "We were taking the wounded off the field when I saw the archer." He tapped his hand against his leg, thinking on the battle. Suddenly, his hand was warm and still. Chloe had taken his hand in her tiny palm and held it close.

"I yelled and pulled my sire to the ground. He was unharmed. I took the arrow in my eye. All hell broke loose. As I was guiding the king to safety, soldiers ambushed us. I fought badly. 'Twas hard to see out of one eye, and my balance was off."

"But you saved him again?" She was breathless.

"Aye. The last two soldiers and I battled. I ran one through. The man fell atop me, and the last one went for the king. Somehow I rolled away and cut the man's legs from under him. My sire was safe. The Scot and I rolled down the hill, and I landed in the fire. 'Twas Garrick who pulled me free, but the damage was complete."

He touched the old scars on his face, remembering the agony.

"The king awarded me Bainford and a minor title." He did not know why he told her, only that he did not want any secrets between them. He had seen what secrets could do. How they had torn Garrick apart from the woman he thought he loved, until she betrayed him. How his father betrayed his mother.

"'Twas a great honor from my sire." He pulled his cloak around her. And, unable to resist, he twisted her curls around his fingers, over and over.

"A healer did her best, but the pain was more than I could bear. When I was no longer screaming and could move about, my sire sent me home. My leg was badly injured, as was my arm. They did not heal properly, and pain me constantly." He sounded bitter but could not help it. "I was no longer able to fight, was no longer needed."

"A lady my grandmother knows walks stiff like you when she gets up from a chair."

"Aye. I am in pain always. Some days my head and eye ache so, I am sick with the pain."

"That's why you were in such a bad mood."

He chuckled. "I have been in a foul temper since I lost my eye, bellowing and stomping about—until you appeared in front of me. You have much improved my temper, brought light into the darkness.

I am truly sorry for what I said. 'Twas in anger and I did not mean them. Can you forgive me?"

"Yes. I forgive you. I said things I didn't mean either. Will you forgive me too?"

"I already have. Truly, I am sorry."

"I should not have fired your servants. It's just I couldn't bear for them to say such ugly things about you. To cross themselves like idiots."

"Aye. Garrick told me you were most fearsome." Chloe had been angry for him, had done what she did *for* him, not against him. Saints, he had found the only woman in the realm who cared naught for his ugliness.

Richard blinked to clear the sight in his good eye. "There is one other thing you should know."

"Tell me." She sounded sleepy in his arms.

He swallowed. "'Tis why I was so angry. The thought of losing Bainford. Of not being the lord. I am a bastard. I would never have risen to lord."

"I'm sorry," she said. "There's something you should know about me. I am also a bastard. Though in my land we call it illegitimate, or born on the wrong side of the blanket. It sounds nicer."

Chloe was like him? Richard needs think on what she had told him. There was much he wished to ask her, but she yawned, almost asleep. His questions would keep until the morn. "'Tis dark out. We will sleep here this night."

She snuggled into him and fell asleep with a sigh. Careful not to wake her, he kissed her on the forehead, content for the first time in his miserable life.

CHAPTER 20

FOR THE FIRST time since he'd sent her away, Chloe was warm. She yawned and stretched, hitting something hard.

She opened her eyes to find Richard looking down at her. Their eyes met, the conversation between them coming back to her. He had darker flecks of blue in his already dark blue eye, which right now was totally focused on her.

"Sorry about that. How's the nose?"

The corner of his mouth lifted in a half-smile. "I daresay it looks better now than it did before." He gingerly touched his nose.

While she wanted nothing more than to wile the day away with him, to get him to open up, she wanted to go home.

Chloe sat up. Home. But she'd meant Bainford. The thought had her chewing her lip. Was it disloyal to her family to want to stay? She snuck a look at him. Did he even want her to stay?

Garrick stuck his head inside the hut. "My arse is frozen. Shall we ride for home so I may find a wench to warm it?"

Outside, the morning sun turned everything into a magical land of snow and ice. Icicles hung from the trees, glinting in the light. The unblemished snow looked like the domain of an ice princess.

"It's beautiful," she said.

"Aye," Richard said, but when Chloe looked at him, he wasn't staring at the landscape—he was looking at her. All of a sudden, she was warm again as she tried her best to smooth her curls.

"Leave them be. I like the way they fly about." He lifted her up on the horse and then settled in behind her, wrapping his cloak around both of them.

"I am glad you are well, mistress." Garrick rode alongside them. "We were worried for you." Then he smirked.

She looked back to see not only Garrick but most of the men with grins on their faces. "What's so funny?" she asked.

"Falconburg is to the north and the west," Richard said.

"I know that," she retorted.

"You went south. Several miles south," Garrick said between laughter. He and the men laughed, and even Richard joined in. But when Chloe laughed too, Garrick tilted his head. "You are not vexed?"

"I went the wrong way. I really am a Merriweather." Seeing the confused looks, she elaborated: "All the Merriweathers are bad with directions."

Garrick and the men looked lost, but she felt Richard shift behind her.

"I understand," he whispered in her ear.

Chloe had made one decision during her time in the past: she was going to learn to ride. Horses were much faster than walking. Plus, they were cute.

Warm from Richard's body and both their cloaks, she dozed on and off, reliving the major moment they'd shared, when he'd come for her and swept her up in his arms. It was almost enough to make her believe her fairy tale had come true.

The gruff man had apologized. And not some halfhearted apology she'd heard guys at school give their girlfriends when they just wanted to move on with their day, pretending whatever the issue was had never happened.

Now that she knew he was illegitimate, his overkill of temper made sense. She'd heard her granda talk about his time working in the casino in Vegas. How men defined themselves by their careers, or titles, or wealth. To a man who'd come from nothing, Bainford was something he'd do almost anything to hold on to.

All his stomping about had rubbed off on Chloe. She rather liked grumbling a bit. It was exhausting to pretend to be happy all the time. Nothing made her madder than when someone told her to smile. Or said, "You'd be so pretty if you smiled." It made her want to punch them.

She could be perfectly content sitting in the library, reading or studying, and then someone would tell her to smile or ask what was wrong. As if they cared; they just wanted the drama. It made her want to throw something. But not a book. The horror. Throwing a book was as bad as the monsters who dog-eared the pages. She shuddered.

"Are you cold?" he said in her ear.

"I'm warm, just anxious to be home."

When they crossed the drawbridge, she wanted to jump off the horse and run, but forced herself to stay seated and not startle the big black horse. All of the kids had lined up in the courtyard, waiting. When Richard lifted her off the horse, they swarmed her, talking at once, so many little voices that she couldn't keep track of who was chattering.

"We thought you'd been eaten by a wolf."

"Or gored by a boar."

"Where did you go?"

"Did you stay with the faeries?"

"Why did you leave us?"

"My lord has been in a foul temper since you left us."

That one penetrated her brain. "What? I didn't leave. Lord Bainford threw me out." While she'd forgiven him, she wasn't above making him suffer and throwing him under the bus.

There were gasps and glares. "Nay."

"Yes, it's true." Then she let it go, not willing to hold a grudge. "But he apologized and all is forgiven."

As she said it, she looked at him with his hood down. His gaze found her and held, and the voices of the kids faded away until there was only them and the lightly falling snow. It was like one of those Hallmark movies her mom loved to watch over and over again.

A tug on her dress snapped her out of the moment.

"Come see. While you were lost, we cleaned the cellar and the chapel."

Chloe hugged Garrick and smiled at the guardsmen. "Thank you for coming for me."

When she hugged Richard, she found herself inhaling the scent of him, warm and comfortable, until someone cleared their throat.

They awkwardly pulled apart. As she let the children pull her along to show her what they'd accomplished, she touched his hand, feeling the calluses on his palm as she passed. "I hoped you would come find me."

He grunted. From him, the grunt was almost a declaration. He might as well have broken out into song and dance.

She giggled, skipping along with the kids through the snow as they chattered away, dogs following along, tails wagging. And the cats? Two of them stood sentinel at the door, disdain on their cute little black faces. The only thing that would have made her homecoming even better was to have her family with her.

At the doorway, the dogs' tails quit wagging, and they moved slowly, looking from one cat to the other. Chloe couldn't hold in the laugh. Sara Beth's cat ran their household. They had a labradoodle who was afraid of the cat, and the cat, Boots, knew it. She would walk up and stare at Pumpkin, and the dog would move back, sit, and wait, while Boots ate the dog's food. Chloe was convinced the cat didn't even like dog food and only did it to show she was boss.

Kind of like Richard. In her time, he wouldn't be expected to be a grownup. But here? He was a man, had been for years. Responsible for a home and all who depended on him. He was so much more mature than her.

She wasn't flighty, but she was only eighteen. The thought of running a household was foreign to her. Enough that she'd acted without thinking. It was hard living in the past. Actions had consequences. And not silly ones, like someone getting mad on social media, but life and death. In the future, she'd be more careful of what she did and said.

After praising the children for the great job they'd done cleaning, she ran into Tomas.

"My lord demanded a hot bath for you, mistress." She followed him to the bathing chamber, pressing her lips together so she wouldn't laugh at how serious he was. While she was waiting for the servants to finish filling the bath, a hearty stew and bread with butter, along with a goblet of spiced wine, was brought to her. Chloe sighed with pleasure as her belly grumbled.

After her bath, she'd changed into a tunic and hose and was curled up in a chair before the fire in Richard's solar. There was a lady's solar, but it still needed repairs.

RICHARD STRODE IN, pleased to find Chloe in front of the fire. She belonged there, in his solar. His lady.

"I have wine." She rose and poured him a goblet.

He groaned and joined her, lying down on the floor. The ache in his back was worse today. Lying on the floor eased the pain.

"Might you continue your labors?" He looked at her through a lock of copper hair that had fallen over his good eye. "The lads all say how nice it smells. The rushes are not slimy or smelly. Even the dogs smell nice."

Chloe made a noise in the back of her throat, sounding rather a lot like him. Which pleased him more than he thought it would. Careful not to smirk, he waited for her answer.

"The girls bathed the dogs. I heard all about it."

"Aye. The lads as well."

"With threats of violence." She stretched. "Yes. I'll stay." Then she curled her hair around a finger, over and over, bewitching him. "Richard?"

"Aye, love?"

"Has there been any word from Falconburg?"

Chloe had not forgiven him. She wished to go to her kin. To leave him.

CHAPTER 21

"Nay, Chloe. No word from Falconburg. 'Tis a treacherous time for travel," Richard said gruffly.

Chloe had accepted that it might be several months before a reply came from Falconburg, but she'd asked anyway, hoping to meet her great-aunt.

After her adventure, she knew trying to make the journey alone would be dangerous. In the meantime, she'd make the best of things, make herself useful, and soak in every detail for when she went home and told her family about her trip. But if she couldn't go back...or decided not to...?

The lack of the familiar sharp pain in her heart startled Chloe. She knew how worried her family must be. Had they even considered she'd traveled back in time?

When she was little, she'd told them she was going to go back and meet her great-aunts. Who knew it would come true? If only she could get a message to them. Gram had told her how the not knowing was the worst. First when she'd lost Granda, and then later when her nieces disappeared.

For the first time since arriving a few weeks ago, Chloe was conflicted. Going back to the future meant leaving *him*.

He was the first guy she'd met who was quieter than her. At first he'd terrified her, but now she tried to get him to talk. And when they sat in front of the fire, like tonight, the silences were comfortable, not awkward, like when she'd gone out with a friend of Sara Beth's current crush. It was a disaster. Dating was hard. Being with Richard was easy, except when he was being a pigheaded idiot.

The days fell into a routine. Chloe would get up and eat, then gather the kids to do chores, with treats awarded at the end of the week for whoever did the best work.

After dinner, she and Richard would walk and get to know each other better, and then she'd take a nap or play with the animals until supper. They would talk, and occasionally Richard would laugh. After supper, she had been teaching the kids the alphabet. Later she'd teach them to read if she was still here. It kept her occupied until it was time to go to bed. He would escort her to her chamber, linger outside the door…but Richard still hadn't kissed her. What was he waiting for? Maybe he only liked her as a friend?

It had been raining all day, so she and a few of the kids had been busy exploring every nook and cranny of the castle from top to bottom. Chloe's stomach rumbled.

"We missed dinner." Wade looked forlorn.

His sister, Maron, sniffed. "Aye, but I smell supper."

"I do too." Chloe grinned. "Come on, I'll race you." And she set off running down the hallway, the kids on her heels.

They skidded to a stop in the hall and went to their places at the tables. Richard stopped cutting his meat and sniffed. "What have you been doing? You reek."

She discreetly sniffed and agreed, but wouldn't give him the satisfaction. The man still had atrocious manners. "That isn't a very nice thing to say."

He reached up and wiped her cheek. "Nay? 'Tis true. You are covered in dirt. Have you been playing with the piglets again?"

She stuck her tongue out at him, happy when he chuckled. "If you must know, we were exploring. You'll never guess what we found."

She pretended she was extremely interested in watching the kids while she waited.

His nose touched her ear, making her jump. "Tell me," he said so low that only she could hear. His deep voice sent shivers through her. He sounded like one of her favorite country singers, Kane Brown.

"There is a hidden room on the fourth floor near the tower." She turned to face him.

He frowned. "I have not found such a chamber."

"Of course not; it's a secret room. Robin leaned against the hearth, there was a click, and the wall opened up." She was so excited that she could hardly stand it.

"Truly?"

She rolled her eyes. "Aren't you excited? Don't you want to know what we found?"

This time he smiled. "Gold."

"No. But almost as good." She was starving, so she took a few bites of the meat, making him wait while she chewed, enjoying watching him fidget. She swallowed then took a leisurely sip of wine before he put a hand on her arm.

"Tell me. Do not make me wait." He was wearing a chestnut-brown tunic and hose that made the copper stand out in his hair. Even with the scars, he looked like a fallen fae prince. Chloe barely noticed them anymore.

"We found several tapestries and a few pieces of furniture. But only one rug." She sighed. "I was hoping for a few more rugs. The floors are so cold."

"Rugs cost money. I will not squander hard-earned gold for pretty trinkets."

"Hair ribbons are trinkets. Rugs are not. You should be comfortable. Your hall doesn't have to be as dismal as your mood." She glared at him. "Big jerk," she mumbled.

"Jerk?" he said.

"Oh, you heard that?" She smiled sweetly. "What is it you say? Oh, right. You're a dolt."

The corner of his mouth twitched, and she knew he was trying not to laugh.

"Respect your elders."

She snorted. "Well, bless your heart. You certainly act like a cranky old man."

Richard leaned back in the chair. No one ever teased him, so she made sure to do it on a regular basis.

"And you, mistress, act like a child."

She rolled her eyes. "That's the best you've got? I'm supposed to be silly and have fun. I don't have to be serious until I finish college and get a job." She clapped a hand over her mouth. Darn it, sometimes she still slipped.

One of the dogs had picked that moment to chase the cat under the table. In the ensuing commotion, Chloe hoped Richard had missed the slip. They good-naturedly sniped back and forth until supper was over.

♨

"RICHARD. Did you hear? There's going to be a market in the village tomorrow. Can we go?"

Chloe liked to sleep late, so he was surprised to see her up and about. She had tied a green ribbon around her hair. She wore her burgundy gown and was holding one of the cats in her arms. The wee beast yawned, showing its teeth, its tail twitching as it watched him.

"Why?"

She stamped her foot, sending the cat running. "It's been too cold to go outside. I'm bored. I want to see people. And I need things." Chloe held up her hands. "I'm not saying I want to spend all your gold. I know how hard you have worked to earn it. I've seen the men that come to fight."

Did she think him unable to best those men? He could win with one hand tied to his belt. He wanted to kiss her as she stood in front of him, tapping her booted foot on the floor.

"Living in a pleasing home improves the mood," she said.

"It does, does it? Says who?" He snorted.

"Everyone, silly." She frowned. "We need wooden serving utensils, a few more spices—you know, stuff."

Richard avoided the village. "Garrick will take you."

"I thought it would be nice to go together." She touched his arm, her delicate fingers sending warmth through him.

"Nay. I have things needs seen to."

His woman narrowed her eyes. "The villagers just need to be around you. They will see you are a man. Not some supernatural being or devil."

She paced back and forth in his solar. "Your face is healed. Look in the water and see for yourself, it is not nearly as terrible as you think." She said it so softly that he took a step closer to hear. "The scars have faded."

He sneered. "I care not what those gossips say. I am the lord of Bainford."

She sighed. "Whatever. I'll go with Garrick."

When she left, he did not feel as pleased as he thought he would. Nay, his heart ached.

CHAPTER 22

"MISTRESS CHLOE, WHAT AILS YOU?" Garrick sheathed his sword and strode over to her.

"That odious man." She plopped down on the stone bench against the wall. It protected her from the wind, and she could watch the men practicing in the lists.

"Ah, Richard." Garrick sat beside her.

"He makes me madder than a wet hen." She huffed.

He threw back his head and laughed. The guy was huge, with enormous hands and feet. Sturdy like an old tree. She wondered why he hadn't married but didn't want to pry into his business. Though she thought he'd make someone a good husband, and the kids adored him.

He slapped his knee. "I believe a hen that is wet would be vexed indeed."

They sat for a while as Garrick explained the finer aspects of sword fighting, pointing out what the men would do next. When they would parry and when they would lunge.

"Garrick? Can you tell me how much money I have?" She pulled the pouch out of her pocket and dropped it in his palm.

He opened it, his eyes wide. "This is a fortune. Where did you get the funds?"

"My father gave it to me to hide on the ship, so I had it when we were in the storm." She hated lying, but there was no way she was telling them she was from the future. If some guy showed up in Holden Beach saying he was from the past, he'd be locked up for a psych eval. No one would believe him. And she had no desire to be drowned or burned at the stake.

"What do you plan to do?" Garrick asked.

"I told Richard I would pay to live here but he wouldn't hear of it, so I want to buy paint for the walls, a couple of rugs, and maybe a few chairs. If I have enough?"

"You have more than enough."

"Don't tell him. I want it to be a surprise."

Garrick looked unsure but nodded. "He does not care for surprises."

"Well, he'll just have to get over it."

"I will take you." He stood. "Now leave me to the lads."

That evening, after supper, Chloe was in the solar with Richard, sitting on the floor on the single rug she'd found in the hidden room. It was beautiful, with muted shades depicting the forest and wild animals. She'd placed the rug in front of the fire, but not so close it would get burned by the sparks.

A couple of dogs of indescribable breed slept on one side, while two of the tiger-striped cats lounged on the hearth. One was close enough to get his fur singed, but he didn't seem to mind.

Sore from spending the day cleaning, she groaned as she wiggled her toes.

Richard took her foot in his hands, rubbing the arches, making her sigh in pleasure.

"Rest. You have been working like the lowest servant when you should fill your days like a lady."

She petted a black dog who was snoring in his sleep. "I can't embroider or sew. I'm useless at cooking. The gardens and orchards are covered in snow. What am I to do with my time? It feels good to accomplish something. To look back at the end of the day and see a chamber sparkling and clean. I'd rather be useful. Otherwise, I'd be lazy and get fat."

The awful man ran his fingernail along the bottom of her foot, making her giggle. He knew how ticklish she was. Chloe wiggled her foot, and he took the other in his hands and rubbed out the stiffness.

"Now, if you had a library, then I'd be curled up in front of the fire reading all day, doing nothing else."

"You enjoy reading?"

She sighed. "More than anything in the whole world."

It was late when he escorted her to her chamber. They lingered at the door until one of the guardsmen cleared his throat. The men and older boys had taken it upon themselves to make sure Chloe was properly chaperoned. She wanted to laugh when they told her but, seeing their looks, knew it would hurt their feelings, so she nodded and thanked them. Though at times like this, she wished they'd leave them alone. Richard would never kiss her with all this traffic in the corridor.

"I will take you to the market on the morrow," he said.

She threw her arms around him, hugging him tight. "Thank you."

The guard cleared his throat again and leaned against the wall, arms crossed. Richard rolled his eyes. "I bid you a good night, Chloe."

"Good night." She shut the door and threw the bolt. Then she stood there with her ear to the door, listening. It was a while before she heard the sound of boots on stone.

RICHARD HAD LEFT Garrick to guard Bainford. He had decided to take Chloe to the market. It had been more than two years since he last visited the village. He wore his hood pulled tight around his face.

Chloe talked and talked, oblivious to his discomfort. She was happy, smiling and laughing, and promising the children she would bring them back sweets. Three lads and three girls ran ahead of them. They had helped Chloe the most the past se'nnight, so she had picked them to come to the market, with the promise of bringing whoever worked the hardest to the next market. She was shrewd.

He was so busy watching her that at first he did not hear the words. 'Twas Chloe's hand in his that alerted him to trouble. She was squeezing his hand so hard that he thought his finger would break.

They were causing a commotion, the villagers whispering and crossing themselves as they passed.

"Please. Ignore them." She tugged on his hand, knowing he was ready to bolt.

He scowled at the men who were suddenly busy looking at their feet. She was pulling him from vendor to vendor, and then she stopped. "I have things to do."

"Aye. I will escort you."

But she shook her head. "No. It is womanly stuff."

He did not let her know how her words wounded him. She did not want to be seen with the beast. He could not fault her.

"As you wish. Find me when you are ready to leave," he said stiffly.

"Thank you." She squeezed his hand and was soon having speech with an old woman selling trinkets. The children were darting to and fro, and Richard scowled. He touched the hood. Should he put it down? Let them see how terrible he was?

But he did not. Unable to bear the gaze of the villagers, he did not speak to anyone until he came to a vendor selling books.

"Good...d...day to you, m...my...lord," the man stuttered.

"I am in need of books. For a lady," Richard said.

The man showed him fine volumes. They were expensive, but Richard knew she would treasure them. He purchased three. A gift to beauty from the Beast of Bainford.

Richard would not come to the village again. He would retreat to his castle to hide his visage from prying eyes.

❦

RICHARD KNEW he had been ill-tempered during supper, but he could not help but remember the look she gave him when she wished to go off on her own at the market. To not be seen with him. He trudged out of his solar, grumbling to himself, only to stop and gape.

Chloe was high above his head on a ladder using a long pole with a cloth on it, scrubbing his walls. Then she would dip the rag in a bucket and repeat the process while the lads called out encouragement.

He did not dare shout at her and have her fall. Four lads were holding the ladder; the rest of the imps were busy scrubbing the walls and floors.

When she scrambled down the ladder, he thought he would swoon, worried she would fall and break her neck.

"Chloe. What are you about?"

She blew a curl out of her face. "No offense, but it's awfully dreary in here. I thought... That is, most homes of this size are painted inside. I thought we should paint all the rooms." She smiled at him, her teeth so white and straight, her eyes sparkling, the color of fine whiskey.

"Paint?" He looked around the hall and noted buckets of color. A few steps closer and he saw burgundy, gold, and emerald green. "Where pray tell, did you procure paint?"

The side of her nose had a smudge of dirt, she was wearing his old tunic and hose, and he thought she looked most fetching with her hair tied back and dirt on her face.

"I bought it from one of the merchants. It was nice of you to take me to the market yesterday."

"Lads, go to the kitchen. Merry made pie." They were gone before he'd finished speaking. "Where did you get the gold to pay for all this?"

She rolled her eyes. "Typical man, only listens to half of what I say." She stirred the paint and smiled. "I told you, remember? It was my parents'. They gave it to me on the ship. When we were shipwrecked, I still had it."

Richard narrowed his eyes. Aye, she had told him the sad tale, but why did he not believe she was telling the truth?

Unwilling to make her angry, he looked at the paint. "'Tis pretty." He proffered his arm. "Come. I have a surprise for you."

She clapped her hands together. "I love surprises."

In his solar, he made her close her eyes and hold out her hands. Then he put the wrapped bundle in her outstretched palms.

"Now open your eyes."

"Books. Oh, thank you!" Her eyes shone in the torchlight. She reverently opened each one. "Poems. Oh, a tale of knights and courtly love, and one about gods and goddesses." She kissed him on the cheek. "These mean everything to me. Thank you so much."

"I am glad you are pleased." He laid the books on a table. "Now come sit in front of the fire. You are cold and your hair is in knots. Margery?"

A little girl came running. "My lord?"

"Fetch me the comb for Mistress Chloe's hair. She has been rolling around with the cows again."

The girl giggled and scampered out of the solar. She was soon back with the comb and ale.

Richard gave Chloe a cup and pulled her onto his lap. He combed her hair in front of the fire, working out each knot, admiring the colors, wrapping each curl around his finger. Her hair was so soft and smelled of winter.

He could find peace with her. Mayhap, in time, she would come to care for him?

CHAPTER 23

THINGS HAD BEEN GOING SO WELL. The hall and several other rooms were painted and cheery, she'd gotten the kids into a routine, and then there was Richard.

They spent a great deal of time together. In the evenings, they'd sit by the fire; she would read, and he liked to brush her hair—so much so that she'd finally come to love her crazy curls instead of being annoyed by them.

He'd even left his hood down the last time a merchant arrived, so he was making progress. Chloe had been in the stables, petting the horses and a couple of the cats, and when she came out, the sun was doing its best to shine.

There was so much beauty around. As much as she missed Holden Beach and the sound of the ocean, she'd come to love it here. The land, sleeping for winter, waiting to be awoken by a kiss from spring, all stirred something deep within her soul.

She'd made her way up to the battlements. The guards were used to her presence. As she looked out at the forest, she knew. "I could stay in a place like this."

The thought was banished just as quickly. She had to go back. With no idea if time passed the same here as it did in the future, Chloe wanted to be with her family. Her grandparents had turned eighty this year, and while people lived longer in her era, who knew how much time they had left?

It was almost like she could feel the stones calling her, a sense of urgency to go home. Could she even go back? Granda said it was possible if the fates were favorable, but her great-aunts never returned. And Chloe didn't know if it was because they'd found their one true love or because they couldn't go back and had made a life here in the past.

She walked for a while longer, deciding she needed to go check on the painting progress on the second floor. If one of the boys had painted the cat or dog again, she'd have their heads.

Later that afternoon, she was on her way to the solar to read for a little while before supper when she heard voices. It was something about the tone of the voices that made her stop and listen.

Chloe knew she shouldn't eavesdrop, but it was Garrick and Richard, and they were being quiet enough that she knew something was up...so she crept closer and listened at the partially open door, hoping no one would catch her.

"You are a lord now. Take Chloe to wife. Get her with child so you have heirs." Garrick's deep voice rumbled out the door. It was a bit soon, if you asked her, but no one did, so she leaned closer to hear what Richard would say to that idea.

"She turns out my servants, thinks I cannot fight my own battles, distracts me until I do not know if I have put hose on, so I look to see. That bothersome wench has disrupted my peace. Rearranged my home, painted the bloody walls in cheerful colors. It was quiet before she came. I do not want her here. As soon as the messenger arrives, I will send her to Falconburg and be done with her for good."

She clapped a hand over her mouth to cover her gasp. A tear trickled down her face to tickle her chin. So that was how he really felt about her. Shaky, her stomach turning over and over, she fled to her chamber and threw herself on the bed.

He didn't want her here, had been humoring her all this time.

Flirting with her for what? Practice for a woman he'd marry? Not some silly girl like her?

The urge to leave was so strong that she'd packed half her belongings when movement at the window caught her eye. It was snowing again. Why had she thought snow was pretty? It made it impossible for her to travel. She'd never make it almost two hundred miles to Falconburg.

What he'd said hurt more than she thought it would. When she was sixteen, she started dating, had even thought she'd been in love, but it had never felt like what she'd felt with Richard. He got her—didn't think she was too quiet, or didn't smile enough, or wasn't pretty enough. She thought he'd accepted her for her. That, with his scars, he'd learned to look deeper than the outside. How wrong she'd been.

There was a knock at the door, and one of the girls stuck her head in. "I'm to fetch ye for supper, mistress."

Chloe didn't turn around. She didn't want the girl to tell anyone she'd been crying. "Could you bring a tray to my room? It's my womanly time, and I want to go to bed early."

"I will tell my lord and I'll bring you some spiced wine with your supper."

"Thank you." Chloe wiped her eyes, wishing she had her phone and could call Sara Beth to tell her what had happened. They discussed in minute detail everything their boyfriends said, looking for hidden meanings or hashing over an argument or something nice that was said. There wasn't anyone here she could talk to about Richard.

"Where is Mistress Chloe?" Garrick asked Richard.

He finished chewing. "'Tis her womanly time." He shuddered.

Garrick blanched. "We will leave her to rest." Garrick drained the cup of ale and refilled it. "It has been more than three years, and your visage is still ugly. Then again, you were always ugly, but the scars are not so terrible nowadays."

"I will not be jeered at. Think you I don't know what is said about me? The wicked Beast of Bainford?"

Richard stabbed the knife into the table, glad Chloe didn't see him do it and scold him for his lack of table manners.

"Do you know parents tell their children I will come and take them away? That I will cook and eat them? And they say I will send the little ones to my master, the devil, if they do not obey their parents." He scowled, sending a serving girl running back to the kitchens. "I will not see the disgust and revulsion on their faces. I am ruined. Leave me be."

Garrick rolled his eyes. "You are my oldest friend, but sometimes you are an arse. You cannot see what is in front of your face. You have a home, a title, a woman who loves you—"

Richard shoved away from the table. He had lost his appetite and would not hear any more womanly prattle from Garrick.

CHAPTER 24

CHLOE STAYED up late thinking through her options. She knew she couldn't make it to Falconburg. If she knew how to care for a horse, she would have left money for Richard in his solar and taken the animal at first light.

Walking was the only option to get her back to the Rollright Stones. Assuming she could find them. She'd always taken for granted having navigation on her phone no matter where she was, but now? What if she went in a big circle?

"Damn it." She stood on her toes and looked out the window. Why did it have to snow so much? Garrick had told her it was snowing much more this year than the last. Remembering her time in the hut, she threw the knapsack across the chamber and leaned against the bedpost, thinking.

The thought of the men she'd encountered made her swallow. There might be more like them. Or worse than them. It was almost twenty miles to the stones, a long distance to go alone in the dead of winter.

A single kick sent the stool a few feet across the stone floor. Nope, she couldn't leave. She was stuck here until a message arrived from

Falconburg. And who knew how long that would take? Garrick told her messages came when they came.

Tears threatened, but Chloe focused on being mad. She didn't want to cry over a jerk like Richard. He didn't want her here? Fine.

She'd soak up medieval England and entertain herself. When the message came, surely Melinda would send someone to bring Chloe to Falconburg. Family was family; it didn't matter her great-aunt didn't know her. Chloe would explain everything once they met. Then she'd ask Melinda how to go home and hope with all her might that the stones would send her back.

Over and over, she twisted her hair through her fingers, a habit left over from when she was little. The money she had could be used to pay one of the guardsmen to take her to the stones. On horseback, it would only take a couple of days.

Why had she traveled through time in the first place? Was it to meet Melinda? If so, she couldn't go back yet. Chloe believed this was a one-time deal. She wouldn't get another chance to travel to the past and meet Melinda Merriweather. And if she'd been sent back in time for Richard, to help him know he was more than his face, well, look how that had worked out.

That settled it. A trip to the stones was a no go. What was she going to do with herself in the meantime? It wasn't like she had any useful skills. Chloe could cook a few basic things but was used to modern conveniences like the microwave. Fishing? No way; baiting a hook was icky. It was winter, so no gardening. She couldn't knit, crochet, or embroider to save her life. Sewing? She could sew with a machine, but not by hand. Too bad reading wasn't an occupation. The only thing she'd been any good at was organizing the staff to clean while she worked alongside them.

Bleary-eyed from tossing and turning, Chloe was grateful Merry had saved her a bowl of porridge. Once she'd checked on the kids to see how they were coming with the painting, she decided to take the whole day to mope over Richard. He'd made her believe he cared for her, but she knew the truth.

He thought she was a pain in the butt and was only tolerating her until he could send her away. Guess she was flirting practice for when he found a more mature woman. What a jerk.

"A GOOD MORROW TO YOU."

Richard stopped Chloe as she was making her way to the stables. Mayhap she hadn't heard him?

"Are you feeling better? You were missed at supper these past nights."

The blasted woman ignored him.

Garrick chuckled, and Richard scowled.

"Mistress Chloe. Have you come to your senses and decided you much prefer me to Richard?" Garrick said.

Richard would pay him back with his fists.

She stopped. "The stench of that man is more than I can bear." Then she stomped away as Richard discreetly sniffed his person. He did not smell.

Garrick roared with laughter. "What did you do to vex her so?"

"I do not know. It has been three days and she will not speak to me." Richard leaned against the wall, watching her as she stopped and talked to his people, a smile for all. All except him. "Women are shrewish creatures." Richard did not want to tell Garrick he feared she had come to her senses and found him as repulsive as the villagers.

Richard cursed as he finished going over the accounts with his steward. How would he know what he had done if the blasted woman wouldn't speak to him?

Garrick leaned against the wall by the hearth, one booted foot crossed over the other, looking happy. Richard wanted to plow his fist into the man's face.

"Are you going to stand there all eve and smirk at me?"

"I know why Chloe is vexed."

Richard pushed back from the desk. "Do you wish to tell me, or shall I ask the witch in the village?"

His friend snorted. "Not likely you would venture to the village to seek her out." Then he ran his hands through his hair, and the look on his face made Richard sit in the chair, his stomach roiling.

"Tell me, man."

"She heard."

"Heard?" Richard was in no mood. "Spit it out, ye bloody whoreson."

"Mistress Chloe heard you say you wished her gone."

Richard glared, tapping his fingers on his knee. "Do not jest."

"I would not. Mistress Chloe is a fine woman. You would be favored by the fates to have such a lady."

"Think you I do not know?" Richard shook his head. "I never said such about her. She is the best of me."

"Aye, you did," Garrick said cheerfully. "In this very room. You said she is a distraction, a bothersome wench." Garrick drained the cup of ale and smacked his lips. "You said you would be rid of her. Send her to Falconburg." Then he frowned. "You are a dolt."

"Bloody hell. I did not mean any of it." Richard thought he would be ill. The eels he'd eaten at supper were swimming in his belly. When Garrick had jested, said Richard should marry Chloe, Richard could not imagine she would have him, so he pushed the thought away, not meaning for her to listen. Why was she listening at doors, anyway? Infuriating, lovely woman.

"You know when my eye pains me, I am—"

"An arse. A bloody witless dolt," Garrick finished. Then he turned serious. "Before you were injured, you would not have seen her."

"I would have."

"Nay, Richard. Hers is a quiet beauty. You would not."

Knowing Garrick was right, Richard snorted and pushed up from the chair. Had the fates caused him grievous harm so he would find Chloe? Nay, he was being daft.

"Where are you going?"

Richard clapped Garrick on the shoulder. "To beg for her forgiveness. Again."

CHAPTER 25

BY THE FORCEFULNESS of the knock at her door, Chloe knew it could only be one man—so naturally, she ignored him. The pounding stopped and started again. It went on that way for several minutes.

"Chloe. Open this door or I will break it down."

His tone had her scurrying. She knew he'd do it, and she did not want to be without a door.

She flung it open as best she could, given how heavy the darn thing was. "What do you want?"

"Will you let me in?"

She scowled at him. "No. Say what you came to say and then leave me alone."

He shifted from foot to foot. "Garrick said one of the kitchen maids told him you had heard me say that which I should not have said."

"Isn't that just great. Does the whole damn castle know?" She stamped her foot, so angry that she wanted to throw something or scream—or both.

"Nay. I did not mean what I said. My eye ached something powerful, and I thought...I thought you could not care for a man as ugly as I."

She opened the door wide enough to see if anyone else was in the corridor. Satisfied they were alone, she pursed her lips.

"When will you see your scars do not matter to me? You stomp and grumble, but deep down you're a good person. So why can't you get over it?" She was tired of him using his injury and the pain as an excuse to be a brat.

They both stood there, looking at each other, the silence stretching out. He broke it first. "Let me in so I may apologize for being an arse."

"No, I don't think so." She stepped back into the room, her hand on the door. "I wish to read my book. Maybe I will talk to you tomorrow and maybe I won't."

Then she shut the door in his face. Why did relationships have to be so hard?

Leaning against the door, listening to him breathe, Chloe heard him mutter, "Vexing woman. Doesn't she know how much I need her?" And then the sound of boots in the corridor as he walked away.

While Chloe got ready for bed, she thought about Richard. He was the first guy she'd really fallen in love with. The boyfriends she'd had the past few years were fine; they just didn't make her feel everything so intensely.

Last year she'd fallen hard for Noah, thought he was the one, gave him her heart. But he'd stomped all over it after she caught him lying about drinking. She wasn't against having a sip or two while she was underage, but Noah had a problem. He drank until he passed out on the weekends, thanks to parents who were too busy with their own lives to pay much attention to him.

When she'd confronted him, he actually denied it, tried to turn it back on her. Said she was uptight and boring, that everyone drank. It was the weekend and he wanted to have fun. Any excuse to avoid taking responsibility for his actions.

After a huge fight, he'd told her he'd quit drinking. For a few weeks she'd thought they would be okay, and then on a Saturday, when she was supposed to be helping Sara Beth with a project, she'd gone over to his house to surprise him and found him drunk by the pool. He sat there and lied about drinking, right to her face, even when she'd caught him. So she'd broken up with him. It had taken her six months to get over him and longer to trust again. But she knew now that it hadn't been love; it had been intense infatuation, that was all.

After that, none of the guys she'd dated lived up to the stories her granda told her. Maybe it was because Richard was five years older than them. More mature. When she was with him, she felt safe. This was a guy who cared about others, not the latest baseball scores or playing video games or cars. Though he was a bit obsessed with his horses.

And he fought with real swords. No matter how many times she sat on the cold stone bench, she'd never grow tired of watching him in the lists, muscles bunching and shifting under his tunic and hose. He was amazing, and that was saying something, as she'd seen some really good swordsmen in the time she'd been here. The first clang of steel on steel always made her jump, much to Richard and Garrick's amusement.

This relationship? If things fell apart, Chloe knew not only would it break her heart, but she was afraid she'd be ruined for all other guys.

With the bed curtains closed, the room was dark, though she could see a sliver of the banked fire in the hearth. All of a sudden, she sat up in bed.

"Spaghetti on toast." It was December. She'd missed Thanksgiving. Her second favorite holiday after Christmas. It was a big deal back home, with tons of food and the whole day together. Her granda and Arthur argued about football while Chloe, her mom, and Gram listened to music, seeing who could find the silliest song and then singing it at the top of their lungs.

They'd get out the china and silver and eat together. Inside if it was cold and outside if it was warm enough. She loved eating outside at her gram's. Hearing the waves crash against the shore. The colors of the water shifting with the tides.

The first holiday without her family.

Wait. Chloe rubbed her hands together. She had the perfect idea.

CHAPTER 26

"WHAT DO YOU SAY, can we have the feast?" Chloe had been going a hundred miles a minute since she'd woken up.

"Aye, mistress. The figs are costly..." Merry looked uncertain.

"Do not worry. I will buy Richard more if he makes a fuss."

Merry smiled and sent the servants to begin preparations for the first Thanksgiving at Bainford.

Too bad they couldn't have mashed potatoes or the to-die-for cranberry relish Chloe's mom made, but the rest of her favorites? They would come close. Instead of turkey, there would be chickens, pheasant, geese, swans, and...pigeons. Yuck.

"Would any minstrels come to play music?" she asked.

"Music?" Richard gingerly made his way into the kitchens. His leg must be bothering him again.

"For the feast tonight. It's been raining for days and I thought we could use an evening of feasting and merrymaking."

He touched her shoulder, his eyes lingering on her face. "Have you forgiven me?"

Chloe blew out a breath. "I'm still a little angry, but life's too short to go around mad all the time. So yes, you're forgiven."

He stood close enough that she could see his pulse flutter in the hollow of his neck. "I will endeavor not to vex you." He smiled at her, the muted blue tunic and hose making his hair even prettier.

She was wearing her gray dress with the apron over it so the dress wouldn't get dirty while she helped prepare for tonight.

"You will try, but I know you'll tick me off again," she said. "I really wanted music tonight if possible."

For a moment he looked sad, then he took hold of one of the small boys passing through the kitchens. "Tristan, come here, lad."

The boy had black hair and huge brown eyes, he looked to be about eight years old. "My lord?"

"Mistress Chloe would like music tonight at supper. We will have a feast. Would you and your brother sing?"

The little boy's face lit up. "Aye. We sang in the church until we had to leave." And he burst into song, mesmerizing the entire kitchen, who stopped what they were doing to listen to the voice of the little angel.

"That was beautiful," Chloe said when he'd finished. The boy blushed and ran out of the kitchens.

She smiled at Richard. "Thank you." Then she gave him a little push. "Now off with you. I have lots to do today."

He pretended to pout but left her to it.

"Will you show me how to make the figs?" Merry stood at the table watching Chloe.

"Of course. My favorite is cranberry relish, but no cranberries here, so we'll have a fig chutney instead. It's good with meat."

She spent the day bustling about, checking to make sure the hall was spotless for the feast, and trying to stay out of Merry's way.

Chloe had shown her the way she made apple pie after finding some wrinkled apples in the cellar. They had cinnamon, nutmeg, cloves, and ginger, though she was careful not to use any more than necessary.

They were also having carrots and winter squash. Stag and fish for those who might not want fowl. And, of course, cheese, bread, butter, and jam. She had added spices and a bit of honey to the carrots, and they'd even made stuffing. Not exactly like home, but close enough.

If Merry and the girls hadn't kept up a stream of constant chatter,

Chloe would have cried at how much she missed her family. Though she was finally accepting the inhabitants of Bainford as her new family.

There was enough time for her to take a bath and dress for supper. She wanted to look nice for Richard tonight. The rain had tapered off, so she took the opportunity to go for a walk. She'd come to like the cold, brisk air—it woke her up after being in the warm kitchens all day.

It was foggy, the light mist and snow on the ground turning the landscape into a surreal scene. For a minute she had serious déjà vu, a fragment of memory from when she'd woken and thought she was lost in the fog. But then she'd fallen back to sleep. Though when she woke, she was in the past. Was it the same for Melinda and her sisters? Had they too been lost in the fog?

"Ouch."

"Who's there?" Chloe bent down to find two boys and a girl huddled by the gate, half frozen. There was no way the guard on the wall could have seen them through the fog. "Goodness. Why didn't you call out to the guards?"

"We did," one of the boys said, his teeth chattering.

The girl's face was pale. "They didn't hear us."

"Come along." Chloe helped them up and led them through the gates. "Where did you come from?"

They told her the tale, how their parents had died from a sickness and their uncle couldn't afford to feed them. How they'd walked from the north a long time until they heard the beast would take them.

She stopped and bent down to look each of them in the eye. "Lord Bainford isn't a beast, though you might think he is if you don't obey the rules."

They nodded as she led them into the kitchens. Their eyes were round as they took in the plethora of food.

"You are muddy and dirty." Chloe pointed to the corner of the room. "Bathe first and then you can eat."

She wasn't sure they were going to do it—they looked horrified by the idea of bathing in the winter—but they smelled, and she wanted everything to be nice tonight.

To drive the point home, she loaded up three wooden trenchers with food left over from dinner earlier in the day and placed them on the table as the children practically drooled.

"Me first. I'll wash," said one of the boys.

Chloe ran into Richard when she left the kitchens.

"More orphans?" He looked them over as they scrambled to fill the bucket with hot water.

"You're gathering quite the collection."

He shrugged. "They have nowhere to go. I would have faced the devil himself for a bed and food when I was a wee lad."

"You're a good man."

"Nay. I am not, and you would be wise to remember it." He growled at her. Then he took her hands in his, the calluses tickling her fingers. "Though I daresay you have tamed the beast, my lady."

CHAPTER 27

RICHARD STRODE through the hall to tell Chloe the news. She was not in his solar or the kitchens.

"Lad, where is Mistress Chloe?"

"She is in her chamber, my lord."

He patted the boy on the back and took the steps to the second floor, so eager to tell her the news that he did not knock.

"One of the Irishmen plays the lute. He will play tonight and the lads will sing. 'Twill be—"

Richard did not remember what he was saying. She had removed her stocking, her leg was bare, and as he watched, she took a spoon, dipped it in a bowl—the smell of beeswax filled the chamber—then spread it on her calf, applied a strip of cloth, took a deep breath, and ripped it off.

She let out a shriek. He crossed the room in two strides.

"What the bloody hell are you about? Have you injured yourself?" He touched the red spot on her calf. "'Tis smooth as a newborn babe." He stroked the skin.

"Um…well…I was removing the hair from my leg." Her hair was pulled up. He could see the colors of the leaves in autumn in each curl.

He touched her leg again, marveling at how smooth it was. "Why?"

Her eyes reminded him of fine whiskey. Garrick was right: she was beautiful, and he would not have noticed her before, but she had his complete attention now.

Pink crept up her neck and cheeks. "Where I come from, all the women remove the hair from their legs and underarms."

His gaze went to her arms. "Does it pain ye?"

"Yep." She showed him the bowl. "Beeswax and a bit of sugar. But don't worry, I'll buy more."

"Nay, you shall have whatever you require."

"Once the wax is melted, you put it on your skin, press the cloth to the wax, and then rip it off."

He winced.

"I know, right?" She grinned. "It stings for a few minutes, but the pain is worth it."

"If you say 'tis so." He sniffed the bowl. The same scent was on her; the light from the candles and fire turned her skin gold.

"I wanted to look pretty for the feast tonight."

Richard reached out and touched her skin, running his hand up her leg, marveling at the softness. "You are beautiful."

She leaned in, and he could see the flecks of gold in her eyes, smell the wax on her skin. Richard pulled her close.

"My lord, the lads are fighting in the hall." One of the servants leaned against the doorway, breathing heavily.

With a sigh, Richard pulled back. "Aye, I am coming." Though he wanted nothing more than to haul her into his arms and kiss her senseless.

"I look forward to dancing with you after supper."

When he turned and looked back, she was staring into the fire, her fingers to her lips. How he envied her fingers.

❧

CHLOE SOAKED in the wooden tub, grateful it was padded with fabric so she wouldn't get a splinter. It was kind of like being in a rustic hot tub without the bubbles.

She wanted to scream. At first she was mortified he had seen her waxing her legs, but then…he thought she was beautiful.

When he touched her skin, she went weak in the knees. Back home, he would have kissed her at the end of their first date. Here? The anticipation, the build-up, made every moment she was with him full of tension. He'd almost kissed her a few times, they were always interrupted.

It was enough to make her want to pull him into the hidden room and kiss him until she got it out of her system. This was what courting or wooing was all about.

Her granda had told her how a single glance or touch could mean so much. She'd thought he was crazy, until she experienced it herself. Found excuses to run into Richard. To brush her fingers against his. She sighed.

The room smelled like lavender. She'd bought the horribly expensive soap at the market, along with a mirror and cloth for a new tunic and hose for him for Christmas.

This would be the first Christmas she wouldn't be with family. Chloe knew growing up meant not always seeing family for every holiday, but she didn't think it would happen so soon.

What she wouldn't give to see her granda and Richard together.

Two of the girls helped her wash her hair and then dry off. Wrapped in a robe in front of the fire, Maron brushed her hair until the curls were dry and crackled with electricity.

THE MEAL HAD BEEN a huge success. Everyone loved the food, and there'd been a surprise. Richard had her cut into a pie using her spoon, and when she did, live birds flew out of it. Chloe screamed while Richard and the men all laughed. She didn't think she'd look at a pie the same way for a long time.

Tristan and his brother sang while one of the Irish stonemasons played the lute. They sang love songs and sad songs about unrequited love and, of course, battle songs.

When the tables and benches were pushed against the walls, Richard claimed the first dance. Chloe and the other women danced until their feet were ready to fall off, casting shadows on the walls in the torchlight.

"Come, walk on the battlements with me." He pulled her cloak around her and offered his arm.

The frigid air felt so good after all the dancing. The moon was full tonight, turning everything silver. She couldn't have asked for a more perfect night.

Chloe turned to point out a shooting star, only to find him watching her. She froze as he took a step closer, and then another. And then she was in his arms, wrapping her arms around his neck, standing on her tiptoes.

His lips were firm against hers. She could taste the spiced wine, smell the snow in the air as she melted against him.

Chloe had kissed her fair share of guys, but none of them kissed like Richard. If he hadn't been holding her against him, her knees would have given way. A perfect ending to the most perfect night of her life. She wanted it to last forever.

The hiss of a sword from its sheath made her jerk back so fast that she hit her head against the wall.

"Let the lass go, Richard." Garrick and two other guardsmen stood there with disapproving looks on their faces. "'Tis not proper. You are a lord now and she is under your protection."

Garrick offered his arm. "Come along, mistress. I will see you to your chamber."

Richard rolled his eyes. "I will see each of you in the lists tomorrow."

In a daze, she let Garrick lead her to her room. He gently pushed her down on the stool, a grin on his face.

"Good evening to you, mistress."

She couldn't form a coherent thought; she was too focused on the sensations running through her body.

When Lilly came in to help her undress, Chloe had recovered, though she kept replaying the kiss over and over. Talk about amazing.

"You were kissing him and he mussed your hair," Lilly said while she removed the pins from Chloe's hair.

Chloe touched a finger to her swollen lips. "How did you know?"

The girl's eyes sparkled and she stepped closer. "His lordship and Garrick were shouting at each other." She tsk-tsked. "You are to have a chaperone at all times."

A giggle escaped and then another as Lilly brushed Chloe's hair. "What was it like?" She sighed.

"Magic," Chloe said with a smile.

CHAPTER 28

Two glorious weeks passed, days full of kisses and avoiding Garrick and the others who had made a game out of trying to catch them. Picnics in the one tower the workers had finished, rides through the snow, and sitting together while she read and Richard went over the accounts for Bainford.

And then the day she'd thought would never come did.

"Chloe, my love, your kin have arrived." Richard kissed her quickly on the lips, took hold of her hand, and practically dragged her down the stairs and out the door into the courtyard.

"We were visiting Winterforth. Christian and Ashley have adopted a new baby and I couldn't wait to see them. Your missive found us there. We came as fast as we could. Can you believe how cold it is?"

The woman was stunning. A little taller than Chloe, with green eyes and gorgeous red hair. The man with her was almost as scary as Richard. He had a wicked-looking scar that ran through his eyebrow and his eye, stopping past his cheekbone. He was lucky not to have lost the eye. He too had green eyes, but black hair and the nose of an athlete. It was crooked from being broken several times.

"You have to be Chloe. I'm Melinda, and this is my husband, James. To be official, Lord and Lady Falconburg."

It was too much: the hint of the Southern accent that made Chloe homesick. Hearing Melinda was like coming home. Chloe burst into tears. Her great-aunt gathered her into her arms, patting her back.

"Has he treated you badly?" Melinda asked. "James."

The man unsheathed his sword. "I'll take the head of the Beast of Bainford." He snarled at Richard, who unsheathed his own sword.

"Try," Richard said. "Let us see what the infamous Red Knight is made of."

Chloe pulled back. "No. Stop." She looked at Melinda, wiping away the tears. "Richard has been wonderful. It's... I never thought... Nutella on toast."

A look passed between Melinda and James. He lowered his sword and said a bit sheepishly, "To the lists? I've been sorely lacking in skilled swordsmen."

Richard nodded. "Aye. Let us leave them to womanly matters."

Sniffing, Chloe took a deep breath. Seeing Melinda after wanting it for so long filled her with so many emotions that they kept bubbling up and out of her, totally out of her control. "I'm so sorry. You don't understand."

"I think I understand quite well." Melinda had kind eyes. They reminded Chloe of Gram.

"Where are my manners? Gram would shoot me. Let's go inside and talk." Chloe led Melinda to the solar, excited and nervous at the same time. She called for bread, cheese, and wine. When they were alone, she took a deep breath.

"You're the oldest, right?"

Melinda regarded her with an assessing gaze. "I am. But I'm afraid I'm at a loss as to your identity."

She couldn't help it: the soft vowels, the lilt, the eyes like Gram's— Chloe burst into tears again. It was a while before she pulled herself together enough to talk.

"I'm so sorry. It's been a little over a month and a half." Chloe sat on the rug, rolling the goblet back and forth in her hands. "Where to start? I'm Chloe Penelope Merriweather. From Holden Beach."

"Pittypat." Melinda's eyes widened. "Can it be? But how?"

"I'm not a Merriweather by blood. Gram—that is, Mildred—and Drake adopted my mom and I."

"Drake? Who is Drake?" Melinda scooted closer. "Oh, I love a good story."

"Drake is my adopted grandfather. He's married to Mildred... Let me get to them in a bit, 'cuz it's a really good story." Chloe couldn't wait to tell that big ole secret.

"Granda knew some bigwig from New York who dealt in antiquities. There was a document. It was like a menu and guest list documenting a Yule celebration at Falconburg. The king was there. You were all there—it said the Lady of Falconburg joined by her sisters and their husbands."

"The king has not come to Falconburg." Melinda nodded. "When?"

"Next year." Chloe refilled their goblets. She had a feeling they were both going to need it.

"Ah. That's what brought you back? But why didn't you go to Winterforth or Highworth? They're so much closer."

"Only Falconburg was mentioned by name."

Melinda tapped her lip. "So I need to make sure there's a menu and guest list next Christmas so you can find me." She arched a brow. "But I better not list my sisters' homes, in case you go there and miss Bainford."

"Exactly." Chloe couldn't believe she was sitting here talking to one of her great-aunts. She was so happy and excited that she was practically vibrating off the floor.

"Now, tell me how you and your mom met cranky Aunt Mildred." Melinda nibbled on a piece of cheese, her legs tucked under her.

"Gram met my mom in the parking lot of the Dollar Store. She was all alone and pregnant with me, and Gram took her in. We lived with her even after she and Drake found each other again. When my mom met Arthur and they got married, we moved to a house a few rows back. Gram lives in Gull Cottage now. Her sister wanted her to have it."

Melinda tore off a piece of bread. "I cannot believe Aunt Mildred married."

"That's just it. She's been married to Drake since she was eighteen." Chloe grinned at the look of shock on Melinda's face.

"Shut the front door. Spill it. I have to know everything. Oh, wait until Lucy and Charlotte find out."

Chloe busted out laughing. "It's so good to hear another voice from home." She crossed her legs and got comfortable, settling in to tell the tale. "Gram told my mom that losing her sisters and nieces made her look at life differently. She vowed to be kind." Chloe paused, seeing Melinda wipe her eyes. "And then there was the whole Drake thing." Chloe launched into the story, giving Melinda the short version. The rest could come later.

"When Gram was eighteen, she went to Vegas the summer before college, much like me coming to England. That's where she met Drake. After a whirlwind romance, they got married, but then something awful happened. She thought he'd left her, but he hit his head and lost his memory and she couldn't find him.

"Fast forward a million years and he was shot during a robbery at the casino where he worked, regained his memory, and came looking for Gram." It was one of Chloe's favorite stories.

"My mom told me the story so many times. How he had to win her over again, how they'd been married all that time and she never told anyone—she'd kept the ring hidden away, had never gotten rid of it." Chloe leaned in. "Here's the best part." She rubbed her hands together.

"Tell me. You're killing me." Melinda's eyes sparkled, and she took Chloe's hands in hers.

"Drake Gregory vanished in 1335 and ended up in Las Vegas, Nevada."

"Oh my stars!" Melinda yelped.

They spent the morning talking, Chloe telling her the entire story.

"Can you believe Granda bought the police station a helicopter when gram turned seventy-five?"

Melinda laughed. "Aunt Pittypat always made a big yearly donation so she never got in trouble for speeding. I can't believe Aunt Mildred carried on the tradition."

Chloe nodded, tucking a loose curl behind her ear. "I learned to drive in her MG."

"I loved that car." Melinda sighed. "I miss Aunt Pittypat so much. It was awful—we lost her when Lucy traveled through time." She sniffed. "I feel so bad I wasn't nicer to Aunt Mildred. She was so stuffy and cranky all the time. Now I know why. It just goes to show, you never know what someone is going through. Imagine losing your soul mate, thinking he didn't want her, and then not telling anyone? Living with that hurt all your life. No wonder she was cranky. I'm so glad she found her happiness."

Melinda grinned. "Wait until I tell my sisters. They are gonna be so mad they missed meeting you and hearing the story." Melinda took Chloe's hand. "Oh, honey, I'm so happy you're here and part of the family."

They ate dinner in the solar so they could keep talking and catching up. Melinda's husband popped in to check on them. He looked at her the way Chloe sometimes caught Richard looking at her.

When he was gone, Chloe told Melinda the rest. "So when I was almost two, we went to the cemetery. Granda said I went straight to Penelope's headstone and knew she was my 'other grammy.' Here's the crazy part: granda said I told them, 'Soon I go home like them.' That I touched each of your headstones."

Melinda gasped. "I've got goosebumps."

"My mom flipped out until Granda asked me more questions. I told him, no, I wasn't going home like Grammy Penelope and Alice—I was going 'where they are.' And I touched all three of your headstones again." Chloe finished her stew. "They said I whispered away to y'all every time we visited."

It was so nice to be able to talk to someone who understood. Chloe had kept the secret of when she was from ever since she'd arrived.

"When I was growing up, I tried all kinds of crazy experiments to travel through time. Until the year I turned ten, fell off the balcony, and broke my arm. After that, I'd try a few times a year, but nothing ever worked.

"Then I came to England this summer. I sat in the stone circle. I'd given up, and then it happened. I traveled through time, though it was winter when I arrived."

"Isn't that the way?" Melinda said. "You let go of something and then it happens. Charlotte said when I vanished, she knew Lucy and I had traveled through time, so she actually prepped for going back. She was so sure she could do it." Melinda touched her hand. "I'm so happy you're here. I know how much it hurts to know you've left loved ones behind."

"Do you think I can travel through time again?" Chloe asked. "Go home?"

CHAPTER 29

RICHARD LEANED AGAINST THE WALL, unable to grasp what he heard. When he took a step toward the door, his legs gave way and he found himself breathing heavily, sitting on the stone floor.

He had come to fetch the women, heard them talking, and listened at the door like a servant hungry for gossip after he had scolded Chloe for doing the same.

What he heard astounded him. His Chloe, the woman he was in love with, had traveled through time.

'Twas as if he could now believe faeries would arrive at his gates. She was from the future and so was Melinda. By the saints.

The many things Chloe said and did, things he thought odd, were because she was from another time. Almost seven hundred years. He could not fathom the things she had seen. He heard them telling tales of fantastical metal beasts much swifter than horses, flying birds, and endless hot water that was like rain in a bathing chamber.

Fury filled him that she would keep such a secret, betray him after all he had told her about himself. Why would she wish to stay with him when she had such wonders in her own time? She would leave him. He had heard her ask her kin how she could go home. Would she tell him, or would he wake one morn to find her gone?

She had family in her own time who would miss her, and family here. Powerful family to care for her. She had no need of him. James Rivers could arrange a match for her with a proper lord, not a beastly bastard.

All this time, she had not cared for him, only stayed until her family could fetch her. Had made him believe she cared for him. With mere words, she had destroyed him, no sword required. Panic rose in his gorge at the thought of losing her. What it had cost him to risk his heart and love her only to have her rend him in twain. His heart wrenched inside his chest.

⚜

THERE HAD BEEN SO much to tell Melinda, and so many stories to hear, that Chloe hadn't seen Richard since her family had arrived yesterday.

James joined them in the solar for supper. They had decided to take their meal alone so they could keep talking without fear of being overheard. Melinda told her it was a serious thing to be accused of being a witch.

Superstitions ran deep, and Chloe had to be careful of what she did and said, especially with the Hundred Years War beginning and the plague coming. Difficult times made people take actions they might not during times of peace.

When she'd gone looking for Richard to talk to him, to come clean and tell him who she really was, one of the boys said he had gone to see to the men. She was disappointed he hadn't kissed her good night but planned to remedy it this morning. There was so much news to tell him.

"Did you find Richard?" Melinda asked.

Chloe was spitting mad. "He won't tell me what's wrong. All day long he's been stomping about, grumbling and being mean." She refilled the goblet again, blinking at the brightness in the hall. A hiccup escaped. "I finally get to meet you and James, and this is how he acts?"

Melinda covered her hand. "James said he went through the men in the lists and then about wore James out as well." She winked. "But don't tell him I told you. Men are full of pride and he would be embarrassed." She touched Chloe on the shoulder. "Do you think he's worried you'll leave? It's obvious he's in love with you."

"Why would I leave? Bainford is my home. I only asked you if I could go home because I was curious, not because I want to." Chloe blinked blearily. "Do you really think he loves me?"

"Hasn't he told you?"

Chloe shook her head, which sent the room spinning. She gripped the table and took a few deep breaths to make it stop. "No. But he's kissed me. Oh my, that man can kiss."

Melinda grinned. "I remember those days." She helped Chloe up. "Let's go for a walk on the battlements and get some fresh air. I'll tell you all about how I met James."

The cold air had done Chloe a great deal of good. But holy cow, she'd had way too much to drink. Melinda and James had gone to their chamber, as they had to leave in the morning. Chloe's great-aunt had invited her to come with them. Her daughter, Emma, was three, and they'd dared not bring her. A nanny was watching over her, along with a dozen ferocious guards, but Melinda missed her terribly and wanted to be home before Christmas.

Christmas. It was less than two weeks away. Wait until Richard saw his gift.

Then she scowled. *If* he got over whatever was bothering him and talked to her. Otherwise, he was getting rocks.

UNABLE TO SLEEP, Chloe wrapped her cloak tighter and paced the battlements. No way was she ever drinking that much again. Merry had given her a disgusting concoction to drink, but between the potion, the fresh air, and movement, she felt a lot better. Bet she'd have a terrible headache in the morning. Lost in thought, she turned and ran into a wall. A warm wall.

"Sorry." She looked up. "Oh, it's you. Why are you mad at me?" She hiccupped.

Richard looked like he'd been running his hands through his hair. He was rigid, the tension rolling off him.

"You lied to me," he snarled.

She blinked and took a step back, out of the warmth of his arms. "What? I did not."

"The Year of Our Lord 2017," he snapped.

"I meant to… That is… I planned to tell you." She leaned against the wall, glad the guard was at the far end. "It's not exactly something you blurt out. You wouldn't have believed me anyway." Chloe glared at him. "You would have had me burned as a witch."

He leaned down, his gaze burning through her. "I would have listened. I took you in, knowing there was much you had not told me. This…this tale… I told you everything about me, gave you my trust, and you betrayed me with untruths."

"I heard you tell your kin you wish to go home." Then he said softly, his voice choked, "You ripped out my heart with the sharpest of blades. I should have known you are like the rest: you could not love a beast."

The coldness in his face made her flinch. "Richard." She reached out, but he pulled away. "Please. I—"

"Why would you want such an ugly beast? All I have is this pile of stones, a title of the lowest order, and a small amount of gold. What I have, I use to care for my people and repairs to the castle. You could have riches and a match with a husband who is not deformed."

She had just about enough. "Honestly. Listen to yourself. James has a terrible scar and he doesn't go around feeling sorry for himself." Chloe was so mad that she paced back and forth. The guard, seeing her face, turned around and went back the way he'd come.

She poked Richard in the chest. "You call yourself a beast. It's utterly ridiculous. A beast wouldn't care for others. Wouldn't give a flying flip if there were holes in his roof or if those he was responsible for were warm and fed through the winter."

Chloe whirled around and stormed to the door. He followed her down the stairs to her chamber.

"Get. Over. Yourself. Everyone has flaws. Issues. So what if yours show on your face?" Chloe paced back and forth in front of the hearth then whirled around, her hands shaking.

"I'm sorry I didn't tell you, but think about it from my point of view. I had no idea if my only family would get my message and come for me, or if you would throw me out like you did before. Flying metal birds? Metal horses that require no rest? You would have thrown me in the dungeon and never thought on me again."

Richard reached out. "I have been a fool."

"No. I'm tired of apologies." She went to the trunk at the foot of the bed, opened it, and rummaged around, coming up with a fabric-wrapped bundle. She unwrapped the mirror and handed it to him. "Look."

He paled, his lips pressed tight together. "Nay." Richard turned away from her.

A long moment passed, then Chloe laid the mirror on the bed.

"I want to go home. Take me to the stones."

"As you wish," he said quietly, and left the room, shutting the door behind him.

Chloe let the tears fall, sobbing until dawn.

CHAPTER 30

JAMES CLAPPED Richard on the shoulder. "All will be well. The Merriweather women have fearsome tempers. Give her time."

Richard stood stiffly. "Nay. She wishes to go back. To the stones."

"Ah, I see." James looked to his wife and Chloe, who had their heads together, talking in low voices. "That is why she would not return to Falconburg with us." He looked thoughtful. "All is not lost. I almost lost Melinda once."

Richard only nodded, unable to speak. Lord and Lady Falconburg mounted their horses and rode off through the gates.

"Chloe, wait." Richard reached for her hand, but she pulled away unable to bear his touch.

"I'm going home. Take me to the stones or I'll go myself."

He inclined his head. "I'll see to the horses."

CHLOE WIPED the tears away as she packed her meager belongings into the knapsack. Melinda and James had offered to take her with them or to take her to the stones.

When James was busy talking to Richard, Melinda had pulled her aside.

"Be careful, Chloe. My sisters and I don't know exactly how time travel works." She tucked a curl behind Chloe's ear, her gloves soft. "You will find yourself with a choice to make in the vortex, as we call it. You'll only have a moment to make the choice. Choose wisely. You're an old soul, but you're still young. Think hard about what you truly want."

She hugged her tight, making Chloe sniffle. "He loves you, and I can tell you love him. Think about him too. Richard is a warrior, like my James. It can be hard for them to open up, and when they do, they leave their hearts unprotected. They are easily hurt. I understand why you didn't tell him, but I think you have to look at things from his viewpoint as well."

Chloe wiped her eyes. "I don't know if he can see himself as I do." She straightened up. "I'll tell Gram about you and your sisters. I wish I could have met them."

"I'll tell them all about you and about Aunt Mildred and Drake." Melinda mounted the horse. "If you decide to stay, send a message. You are always welcome to live with us or with my sisters. If you do stay, and I hope you will, come visit in the spring."

THE JOURNEY to the Rollright Stones took three days due to the inclement weather. During that time, they barely spoke, each lost in their own thoughts. Chloe felt odd dressed in her jeans and t-shirt, the sneaker mules more brown than white. She kept the cloak on. She'd take it off when it was time.

Over and over she kept going back and forth. She knew she loved him, but was it enough? As much as she wanted to make a life with him, she didn't want to be with a man who felt sorry for himself the rest of his life. What was she going to do?

Still no clearer on her choice, Chloe felt the stones before she saw them. Richard lifted her off the horse and tied the animals to a nearby tree where there was a small patch of grass the snow had not touched.

He handed her the knapsack, but she shook her head. "I decided I won't need the clothes. Keep them. The women can use them."

"As you wish," he said. "I will wait until the morn to make sure you...go safely home." Richard leaned forward and kissed her on the cheek, then he turned and walked into the woods without looking back.

❧

CHLOE DIDN'T KNOW how long she'd sat there looking at the stones, listening to them whisper to each other. It was late afternoon when she stood, stiff from sitting and half frozen. Her heart breaking, she turned to the stone on her right and tripped, scraping her ankle.

When she sat up, the stones in front of her had vanished. The sound of waves crashing against the shore and the smell of the ocean filled her heart. She could hear her family talking and laughing. Could see Gull Cottage as if she were standing on the beach looking up at the house.

Her mom and Arthur were on the porch with Gram and Granda, drinking sweet tea and smiling.

The breeze caressed Chloe's skin, warming her from the inside out. The sun shone down, and she thought about long showers, hot chocolate, days of reading, going to college, and the rest of her life and dreams.

Her family was tougher than she thought. They were fine. It was time to look within to her deepest desires, what she really wanted. The stones whispered, more urgently. It was time.

❧

RICHARD SAT before the fire muttering to himself. He had opened the sack with her belongings, inhaling her scent. Within he found her bag of coin. She had left him her fortune. With a frown, he emptied the contents of the sack on the ground. There was another bundle. He unwrapped it to see the mirror. He did not know how long he stared at the wretched mirror before he picked it up, held it to his visage, and opened his eyes.

The morn passed. He ate a meager dinner and waited, looking to the sky, beseeching the fates. "Name the price and I would gladly see it done."

The day deepened, and he knew. She had left him to go back to her family, all because he could not see past his own ruin. 'Twas too late to tell her how much he loved her, how he now knew he was more, he was whole, and the scars no longer held sway over him. But he had waited too long and lost her.

"Richard."

He unsheathed his sword. The stones played tricks on men. The light was fading as he watched her walk through the snow. 'Twas his Chloe.

"You did not go?"

"No." She wiped her cheeks.

Richard sheathed his sword and ran to her, as she ran to him, arms outstretched. He swung her up in his arms, raining kisses on her face, holding her tight to reassure himself she was real and not a trick of the stones.

"I'm sorry. I should have trusted in you, told you the truth," she said, weeping. "I want no other. I've been searching for someone like you my whole life. Ever since I was small and my granda told me stories of knights and their ladies. Ever since I was a little girl, I knew I would travel through time. My granda was from this time. He's already gone to the future. He told me stories of knights and castles and brave women, though I figured out he embellished parts of those stories. Then I traveled through time and met you. I love you for you. We will grow old, wrinkly, and our eyesight will fail. We'll be hard of hearing and I will still love you. Not for what you look like but because I love you. For what's inside. I love the man you have become because of your injury."

Richard eased them down to sit on a fallen log before he fell. For the first time since he had been injured and lost his eye, Richard wept.

"How long I've wished for a woman to love. One who does not look upon me with revulsion. One who sees me as you do. You have befuddled me, my lady." He wiped the wetness from her cheeks and then his.

"If I was given the choice to keep my visage and my eye but it meant I would not have found you, I would gladly lose them again. Would cut my eye out and offer it to the fates. You are my light in the night sky, guiding me home in the darkness." Richard let himself weep, knowing he had almost lost the woman he loved beyond all measure.

"PLEASE," Richard whispered. And Chloe's heart shattered into a million pieces. All the love songs she'd listened to on the radio made sense. The emotions filled her, burst out of the broken pieces and sliced her to ribbons. Together they would stitch the pieces back together. Love hurt and love healed.

"I've waited my whole life for you. A dragon in the body of a knight. You are the knight from the stories. Fairy tales do come true. I love you with all my heart and soul."

"Forever, my love. Be my moon lighting the way on the darkest of nights."

"Always," Chloe said, and kissed her dragon turned knight in shining armor.

ACKNOWLEDGMENTS

Thanks to my fabulous editor, Arran at Editing720.

ABOUT THE AUTHOR

Cynthia Luhrs writes time travel because she hasn't found a way (yet) to transport herself to medieval England where she's certain a knight in slightly tarnished armor is waiting for her arrival. She traveled a great deal and now resides in the colonies with three tiger cats who like to disrupt her writing by sitting on the keyboard. She is overly fond of shoes, porches, and tea.

Also by Cynthia: There Was a Little Girl, When She Was Bad, and the Shadow Walker Ghost Series.

facebook.com/cynthialuhrsauthor

twitter.com/wickedgreens

instagram.com/cynthialuhrs

Made in the USA
Coppell, TX
25 May 2020